AN AROMA OF COFFEE

Dany Laferrière

AN AROMA
OF COFFEE

Translated by David Homel

Coach House Press
Toronto

Published with the assistance of the Canada Council,
the Department of Communications, the Ontario Arts
Council, and the Ontario Publishing Centre.

Printed in Canada

Coach House Press
50 Prince Arthur Avenue, Suite 107
Toronto, Canada M5R 1B5

FIRST EDITION

Canadian Cataloguing in Publication Data
Laferrière, Dany
[Odeur du café. English]
An aroma of coffee
Translation of: L'odeur du café.
ISBN 0-88910-439-5
I. Title. II. Title: Odeur du café. English.
PS8573.A34804413 1993   C843'.54   C93-094713-4
PQ3919.2.L3404413 1993

For Da, my grandmother
Marie, my mother
Ketty, my sister
my aunts Renée, Gilberte, Raymonde, Ninine
Maggie, my wife
and Melissa, Sarah and Alexandra, my daughters,
this endless line of women who, from night
to night,
conceived and gave birth to me

Great hawks, black companions
of my dreams
What have you done to the land?
What have you done to my childhood?

— J. F. BRIERRE

PART I

1. THE GALLERY

I grew up in Petit-Goâve, a town a few kilometers from Port-au-Prince. If you take the National Highway south, Petit-Goâve is just after the great Tapion mountain. Let your truck (because you will be traveling by truck) coast down to the barracks (painted canary yellow), bear to the left, go up the hill, and see if you can stop at number 88 on the rue Lamarre.

There, you may very well discover, sitting on the gallery, a smiling, peaceful old woman and a ten-year-old boy. The old woman is my grandmother. Call her Da. Just Da. The boy is me. It's the summer of 1963.

BOUTS OF FEVER

When I think about it, nothing much happened that summer, besides my tenth birthday. True, I was sick, I had bouts of high fever, which is why you would have found me sitting quietly at my grandmother's feet. According to Dr. Cayemitte (whose wonderful name is that of a tropical fruit), I was to stay in bed over summer vacation. But Da let me sit out on the gallery and listen to my friends shouting and yelling as they played soccer, next door, in the animal pen. The smell of manure made my head spin.

THE LANDSCAPE

Like the canvas of a naive painter: in the distance, the great bald, smoking mountains. On their slopes, peasants gather dry wood for burning. I can see the shapes of a man, a woman and three children on the side of the old mountain. The man is building a fire only steps from his house, a little thatched hut with a door and two windows. The woman goes into the house, then comes out immediately and stands in front of the man. She is talking to him, waving her arms in the air. Thick black smoke rises into the clear blue sky. The man picks up a bundle of twigs and throws them onto the fire. The flames rise higher. The children run around the house. The woman chases them inside, then walks back to the man. The fire stands between them.

I told Da all about it. It's true. I tell Da everything. Da says I have an eagle eye.

THE SEA

All I do is turn around, and I can see the red sun sinking slowly into a turquoise sea. The Caribbean Sea is at the end of my street. I see it sparkling beyond the coconut trees, behind the barracks.

THE WIND

Sometimes, late in the afternoon, I feel the breath of the trade winds on my neck. A soft breeze that scarcely stirs the dust in the street and, sometimes, the black dresses of the peasant women coming down from the mountains with sacks of coal balanced on their heads.

A YELLOW LIQUID

Once, a peasant woman stopped just in front of our gallery. She spread her thin legs under her black dress, and a strong stream of yellow liquid followed. She lifted her dress ever so slightly and stared straight ahead. The sack of coal did not even move.

I couldn't help giggling.

DOG

We have a dog, but he's so skinny and ugly I pretend I don't know him. He had an accident, and ever since, he has a funny way of walking. As if he were wearing high-heeled shoes, as if he had adopted the careful, elegant walk of old ladies coming back from church. We call him Marquis, but my friends nicknamed him Madame the Marquise.

THE RED BICYCLE

Another summer, and I still won't get the bicycle I've always wanted. The red bicycle I was promised. Of course, I wouldn't have been able to ride it because of my dizzy spells, but there's nothing more alive than a bicycle leaning against a wall. A red bicycle.

FLIGHT

Last summer, I stole a bicycle, Montilas the blacksmith's bicycle, from right in front of his house. The bicycle was leaning against a tree, by the town library. In the shade. The bicycle was just waiting for someone to jump on it and ride south. I climbed on quietly and rode behind the church, all the way to Petite Guinée. There's a little hill you go down. Montilas' bicycle was well oiled. The wind on my chest, my shirt off (I had tied it around my waist), I lost track of time. I had never gone so far in that direction. By the time I returned, the sun was halfway in the sea. Da was waiting for me, standing on the gallery.

YELLOW DRESS

I didn't see her coming. She came up behind me, the way she always does. She was returning from afternoon Mass with her mother. Vava lives at the top of the hill. She was wearing a yellow dress. Like the fever of the same name.

KITE

I watched her for a long time. Her mother was holding her hand tightly. I counted the number of steps it takes her to reach her house. Sometimes she reminds me of a kite flying above the trees. You can't see the string.

THE STREET

Our street isn't straight. It twists like a cobra blinded by the sun. It begins at the barracks and stops suddenly at the foot of the Croix de La Jubilée. A street of speculators who buy coffee and sisal from the peasants. Saturday is market day. A regular hive of activity. People come from the twelve neighboring rural sections that form the district of Petit-Goâve. They walk barefoot, wide-brimmed straw hats on their heads. The mules go before them, heavy with sacks of coffee. Long before sun-up, you can hear the racket from the street. The animals paw the ground. The men shout. The women cry. Da gets up early on Saturday to make them coffee. Strong black coffee.

FISHING

The women sell eggs, vegetables, fruit and milk to buy salt, sugar, soap and oil. My dog Marquis loves to push through the crowd and bring me back a piece of soap or a fish in his mouth. He puts it down next to me, looks up with his soft eyes, then runs off to go fishing again.

THE COFFEE OF LES PALMES

According to Da, the best coffee comes from Les Palmes. In any case, that's what she always drinks. Da can't buy large amounts of coffee, like before. We went bankrupt ten years ago, long before my grandfather died. But the peasants go on offering to sell Da coffee. When they see she doesn't have the money, they leave a half-bag of coffee beans on the gallery. Da looks the other way, and they disappear without being payed. The coffee lasts a week because Da is always pouring a cup for everyone.

PARADISE

One day, I asked Da to tell me about paradise. She showed me her coffee pot. In it was the coffee from Les Palmes that she prefers, mostly because of its aroma. The aroma of Les Palmes coffee. Da closed her eyes. As for me, the smell makes my head spin.

TOBACCO

Every peasant woman smokes a pipe, a short cutty made of baked red clay. They rub big leaves of dried tobacco between their palms to make powder. They smoke their pipes under their wide-brimmed straw hats.

THE BLUE CUP

Da is sitting in a big chair with a coffee pot at her feet. I'm close by, lying on my stomach, watching the ants.

From time to time, people stop to talk to Da.

"How are you, Da?"

"Very well, Absalom."

"And your health, Da?"

"Just fine, thanks to God ... A cup of coffee, Absalom?"

"I won't say no, Da."

Absalom's face as he concentrates, inhaling the coffee. He drinks slowly, clicks his tongue from time to time. The little blue cup that Da keeps for the inner circle. The last sip. Absalom sighs; Da smiles. He gives her back the cup and thanks her with a tip of his hat.

ANTS

The gallery is paved with yellow bricks. Colonies of ants live in the interstices between them. There are little black ants, heedless and gay. Red ants, cruel and carnivorous. And the worst kind of all: the flying ants.

On my left: a dragonfly covered with ants.

NO BONES

My body is elastic. I can stretch it out and shrink it, swell it up or flatten it down, in any way I wish. But, usually, I have a long, boneless body, like an eel. When they try to catch me, I slip through their fingers.

"Why are you fidgeting like that?" Da asks me.

"I want to go."

"You know you're sick."

"Just to watch."

"Only for an hour, then."

I dash off to the park.

THE PARK

It's really an empty lot where the peasants tie up their horses when they come down for the market. Actually, they leave them with old Oginé, whose job is to find them a good spot in the park. He brings them plenty of hay and gives them water to drink when the sun is at its zenith. Most of the horses have sores all over their backs. Oginé rubs down their backs with a brush, then puts big leaves over their open sores. Without flinching, the animals let him tend to them. Oginé is in charge of the park. We give him a little something (money or fruit), and he lets us play soccer next to the animals. The smell of manure turns my stomach every time. I hold onto a horse's neck. The horse's left eye is full of flies, little green flies. I won't leave my spot. I wait for the end of the game.

ANIMALS

Animals are dangerous. You have to be especially careful with those that pretend to be sleeping. Last year, Auguste got kicked in the stomach. It happened at the beginning of vacation. He spent the whole month of July in bed. His mother put dozens of little leeches on his stomach to suck out the bad blood. As soon as she turned her back, Auguste swallowed the leeches, one after the other. Never stand behind an animal. Da tells me that every time I go to the park.

THE GAME

It's almost dark but they're still playing in the park. They won't stop until it's completely dark and no one can see the ball. One time, we kept on playing through the darkness. That's the way it always is at the beginning of summer. You want to see how far you can go.

NIGHT

Da likes to stay up late. Once, she saw Gideon, with his white dog following behind, on his way to the river. That was a month after he died. Da isn't afraid of anything. She even called out to Gideon, who was hiding behind his big straw hat. He murmured something that Da didn't catch.

It had to be Gideon, because his dog was following him.

NIGHT OWLS

Da went inside to make fresh coffee. I think we'll be night owls, this evening. Da will tell me all kinds of stories about zombies, werewolves and she-devils until I fall asleep. When I awake, I'm always amazed to be back in my own bed. I love falling asleep that way, with my head on Da's lap, and she telling me scary stories. One evening, Da asked me to go inside and go to bed a little earlier than usual. She wanted to be alone. I always know when she wants to be alone. But I wanted to be with her, so I pretended to go inside, then I slipped back onto the gallery. I lay down in a dark spot, near the old coffee scale. Da didn't see me. I watched her in the darkness. Her eyes were shining and she was looking up at the sky. As if she were trying to count the stars. Finally, I fell asleep. When I awoke, I was alone on the gallery. All the doors were locked and there was no one in the street. It was the middle of the night. I thought I was in bed, having a nightmare. I stood up; my eyes were open. But that can happen to you in a dream. So I banged my head against the scale to see if it would hurt. But I banged myself too hard.

The pain was terrible. I screamed, and that woke up Da. She opened the door for me. Scarcely had we closed the front door when a horse came galloping past at full speed.

In Petit-Goâve, everyone knows that Passilus changes into a horse after midnight.

THE GALLERY

Around two o'clock on any summer afternoon, Da washes down the gallery. She places a big white tub full of water on one of the trays of the scale, and with a small plastic bucket, she throws the water onto the gallery with a flick of her wrist. She cleans the corners carefully with her rag. The bricks turn as shiny as new pennies. I love lying on the cool gallery and looking at the drowned ant colonies in the spaces between the bricks. With a blade of grass, I try to save some of them. The ants can't swim. They let themselves be washed away by the current until they can grab onto something. I watch them for hours.

Da drinks her coffee. I observe the ants. Time has no meaning.

2. MY NAME

MY NAME

No one knows my name, except for Da. I mean my real name. Because I do have another name. Sometimes Da calls me Old Bones. I love staying up as late as possible. When Da calls me that, I feel like I really am a hundred years old. I asked Da to keep my name secret. My real name, of course.

THE OLD WOMAN

The old chicken-lady comes from a long way away. Da thinks it takes her more than a day to walk to Petit-Goâve. One afternoon, just like that, there she is in our yard. Da goes out to buy a chicken or two from her, and I hide because Da says the woman is a she-devil. She can change herself into any animal, even in broad daylight. You would understand if you saw her red eyes, black nails, crooked fingers, yellow teeth, her hair that goes all the way down to her waist. Every month, she comes to sell chickens to Da. She's never seen me. I always hide as soon as she shows up.

MY SECRET NAME

The old chicken-seller's name is Seraphina. I heard it one day when I was hiding behind the door. She doesn't know my name. Da says that you're at the mercy of anyone who knows your real name. There is one name for the outside world (friends, teachers, girls). Your official name. Then there's a secret name that no one must discover. You choose your name, and you never reveal it to anyone. If you ever forget it, you're finished. I told mine to Da, so if I ever do forget it, she can remind me what it is.

THE ANTS

Do ants have names? They run like crazy through the cracks between the bricks. When they meet one another, they stop for a second, nose to nose, then run off again at top speed. They all look alike. Do they all have the same name?

MY BOTTOM

Da told me that when I was five years old, my older cousins left me on an ant hill, and the ants literally ate me up. I wasn't found until much later, with my eyes bright. I didn't cry. My bottom was red and swollen.

All the ants have big bottoms.

THE MADWOMAN

Naréus' daughter (the skinny one with big eyes) yelled something at the madwoman, then ran into her house and hid. The madwoman went to Naréus and told him everything. Naréus summoned his daughter and gave her a beating on the gallery, in front of everyone.

"Do you know why Naréus did that?" Da asked me.

"Yes, Da. Because she was nasty to the madwoman."

"Naréus is afraid the madwoman will cast a spell on his daughter."

"She can still cast a spell, Da."

"No. By giving her that beating in front of everyone,

Naréus got back his daughter's good angel. Otherwise, the madwoman could have really done his daughter harm. By punishing her in front of everyone, Naréus avoided a second punishment for her, for no one may be punished twice for the same mistake ... Do you understand, Old Bones?"

"No, Da."

"That doesn't matter. One day you will ..."

THE MADWOMAN'S WEDDING

Nobody knew the madwoman before she came to town. People said she was from Miragoâne. According to Simplicius the lottery-ticket seller, she was a girl from a good family who had gotten pregnant by a young doctor from Port-au-Prince interning in Miragoâne. After much hesitation, the young man agreed to marry her. The couple made it as far as the altar. The ceremony went according to plan. At the end, the priest asked the ritual question: "If there is anyone who knows a reason why this couple should not be joined in holy matrimony, speak now or forever hold your peace." There was silence. Then a woman spoke up from the back of the church. "I know a reason." The silence grew deeper. In a broken voice, the priest asked, "Do you know a reason, Madam?" Another silence. "Yes, Father, this man is my husband and the father of my three children." Pandemonium erupted in the church and the bride was never seen again. The story goes back twenty years. According to Simplicius, the bride turned into the madwoman who roams the streets of Petit-Goâve. Loné the notary says that Simplicius' version is but one among many.

THE MADWOMAN'S NAME

No one in Petit-Goâve has ever discovered her real name.

People say The Madwoman, or The Bride. She has no name.
Some people believe she has forgotten her name. Others
maintain that she won't reveal it, to keep her family from
finding her.

Da says she's just a poor woman, and that only she can
tell us her secret.

I have a secret too. But I won't tell it to anyone, not
even Da.

3. THE HOUSE

Ours is a large wooden house, painted yellow, with big blue doors. You can spot it from far away. The roof is made of corrugated metal. New metal. It blinds the truck drivers who take the turn near the barracks. Da is thinking of having it painted black. I'd prefer red. Every time Simon, the big man who drives "Thank You Mary," goes by our gallery, he slows and asks Da when she is going to have the roof painted. And every time, Da says, "Next week, God willing." But it never gets done. Once, Simon said, "Next time I'll ask God, since he's the one who's not cooperating."

Da laughed, as did Simon. I did too.

SACKS OF COFFEE

My grandfather was a great speculator in commodities. He bought coffee from the peasants and sold it to the Maison Bombace. The Maison Bombace is by the harbor. That's where all the speculators go to sell their coffee. At the end of the month, a big boat comes to pick up all the coffee in Petit-Goâve and take it to Italy. The whole town pours down to the harbor to watch the loading of the coffee. I always went with my grandfather. The longshoremen were sweating. People were running every which way, like frightened ants. Men from the Maison Bombace would have the speculators sign all kinds of papers. My heart beat faster every time I saw our coffee sacks go by. They wore yellow ribbons.

THE BIG ROOM

The room looks onto the gallery and the right side of the house. A large room where we used to store sacks of coffee. In better days, they were piled up to the ceiling. My aunts and my mother played there when they were young. Aunt Renée would climb to the top to read her novels. My grandfather hated novels. He said they weren't real life, they were all lies. If you got caught with a novel, your goose was cooked. My grandfather was a tyrant with his daughters. Da always says he shouldn't have had girls. He ended up with five.

THE FIVE SISTERS

Da always says that my grandfather should have had sons to look after the business. To go up to Les Palmes to get the coffee, negotiate with the peasants and their machetes, and transport the coffee to the Maison Bombace. Instead, he had five daughters. Artists, according to Da. Fit for the nut house, my grandfather would retort.

DA'S DAUGHTERS

My mother, the oldest of the family, has brown skin, high cheekbones, soft eyes and a smile that's even softer. Raymonde comes next; she has a screw loose in her head. She dresses in bright colors, and her clothes drive my grandfather crazy. Her long fingernails are as red as oxblood. Aunt Raymonde makes her hats herself, and you have to see her to believe her on Friday evenings, at vespers. Even my grandfather is afraid of her. Da says the devil wouldn't dare sit down at table with her, for fear of being the main dish. She's a born actress who plays sell-out shows for a small but faithful audience. Aunt Renée comes right after her (eleven months separate them). She's very thin with long, black, very black hair, and green eyes. Aunt Renée is as white as a black woman can be without being white. She spends her precious time cleaning her jewelry—a ring, two bracelets and an Oris watch—with cornstarch. Aunt Renée has always had a wasp waist and she grinds her teeth in her sleep. Aunt Gilberte is the nicest and most self-effacing. She has almond eyes and always wears pleated schoolgirl skirts. Aunt Gilberte is morbidly shy. The opposite of Aunt Raymonde. You would never think the two were sisters. Aunt Ninine is the youngest and most beautiful of the sisters. She's black, with shining eyes. Da says she has her father's healthy white teeth. At the end of the afternoon, the five sisters like to sit on the gallery, each in her favorite spot.

THE BREATH OF LIFE

My mother and her sisters waited all their lives for their father to die. "They'll never admit it, but I know it's true," Da says.

"Why, Da?"

"To finally be girls, and not just boys who never made it."

"But they are girls, Da."

"Yes. But your grandfather decided otherwise."

"What do you mean?"

"No one had the right to breathe in this house without your grandfather's permission."

I try to hold my breath to see if it's possible not to breathe. Da looks at me.

"What are you doing?"

"Waiting for your permission to breathe."
Da bursts into laughter.
"That's just a figure of speech."
Da always says that: a figure of speech.

THE BLACK LIVING ROOM

The only mysterious room in the house. I rarely go there. It's always dark inside. With a big oval mirror at the back. On the wall: a reproduction of *L'Angélus* by Millet. A narrow bed for guests near the little yellow screen. This room is always cooler than the others. Sometimes, for no good reason, my aunts throw a little party in the living room. Everyone gets dressed up, they eat Ritz crackers and drink cola and Seven-Up until midnight. Aunt Raymonde is always the chief organizer.

THE YELLOW DWARF

Why, every time I sleep in the living room, do I always have the same nightmare? A tiny woman, no more than thirty centimeters tall, is parading on high heels before me. She looks to be around sixty years old. Her body is well proportioned, but her head seems a little too big for her frail body. She stares at me with her big yellow eyes until I start screaming like a man possessed. When I describe the dream, no one believes me. I'm afraid to go through the living room, even during the day. I always take the side door that opens onto the park.

THE MIRROR

Aunt Ninine likes to fix her hair in the living room mirror. Which means she turns her back to the door, the one that opens onto the park. One day, Da saw old Oginé looking at Aunt Ninine in the mirror. He was making signs with his crooked fingers. Da was sitting in the yard, under the mango tree. She jumped up and ran toward Oginé and grabbed him by the collar. Da pushed him, and he fell onto his back in a patch of flowers.

"Why did you do that, Da?"

"He was going to steal her angel."

"How?"

"In the mirror. She would lose her reflection. He could have captured her soul and put it in a bottle. Ninine would have become his slave. Without the soul, the body is nothing. Do you understand that, Old Bones?"

"Yes, Da."

PRINCE

Da told me the story of Prince. His name was Prince, but he was ugly and poor. He lived near the bridge, by the big cemetery. Prince lived in a hovel, but people said that the most beautiful women in the town would visit him at night. He had stolen their angels. He could do whatever he wanted with them, they, the most beautiful women. Da said that people called him Prince because, despite his ugliness and poverty, he lived like a prince.

PIN

I am the oldest son of the oldest daughter. The first child of the house. The treasure of five sisters. Five mothers. My mother and her sisters sew me little suits in their favorite colors. Blue for my mother, the color of Mary. Aunt Renée loves yellow. Red for Aunt Ninine, blood red (she wanted to be a nurse). Green for Aunt Gilberte. And Aunt Raymonde, my godmother, maroon. Every Sunday, I wear a different colored suit. They spend all week buying the fabric at Elias' store, choosing the pattern from the catalogues, cutting it and making me try it on. My aunts wheel around me like frenzied ants around a bread crumb. I am the center of the world. The day before, on Saturday, they sew my suit—depending on which aunt's turn it is—on the old Singer sewing machine Aunt Renée won in a raffle. My aunts are pretty odd seamstresses, so I always end up with pins hanging off me and sticking me every time I brush up against a door or fall on the ground.

A BIG YELLOW BOW

My grandfather frowns on all this feminine attention paid to my person. He always wanted to make boys out of his girls. And now they're making a girl out of his grandson. My grandfather flew into a terrible rage when he saw a big yellow bow in my hair. It was Aunt Renée's day. They must have undressed me completely and, that day, I was wearing Aunt Raymonde's maroon suit. Aunt Raymonde's day wasn't for another two weeks, but Aunt Renée wasn't ready, so I had to wear the maroon suit. Da says that's my grandfather's favorite color.

A LONG NAP

I never saw my grandfather in the dining room, nor the living room, and especially not in the big room, the women's room. During the day, you could find him in the coffee room, in front. Always sitting by a sorting table I've used to do my homework ever since "the worldwide coffee crash." My grandfather could spend hours there, looking off into space. Now and again, he would brush away a fly that had gotten too close to his mouth. Then he would take up his accounts for the day, which he wrote down in a little schoolboy's notebook. His lunch would be brought to him. He would eat, flattening his rice with his fork. An hour later, he went into the little room for a long nap. My grandfather liked to lie on his back, his head slightly raised so he could look at his roses through the half-open door.

4. ROSES

THE LITTLE BUCKET

My grandfather had but one passion: roses. He had them planted all around the house. He watered them himself every morning and every evening. I would fill a little blue plastic bucket and give it to him. With the bucket, he could water no more than three or four plants. At first, we would work slowly. I loved doing the job with my grandfather. He was always nice to me, he kept asking wasn't I tired, didn't I want to take a little rest? Then I would run faster to fill the bucket. I went faster and faster. My heart beat hard.

FATIGUE

One day, Da asked me to slow down.
"Why, Da?"
"Because he's tired."
"But I'm not tired."
"You're not ... But your grandfather is."
"That's not true, Da. He always asks me if I'm tired ..."
"That's because he's tired."
"Then why doesn't he say so, Da?"
"He did, but you didn't understand."
"He didn't."
"But he did, my boy."
"He didn't."
Da laughed at how insistent I was.

"That's what he means when he asks you if you're tired."

"Then why doesn't he just say it?"

"It's a figure of speech, Old Bones."

TRACTORS

Tractors were my grandfather's other passion. Back in his wealthy days, he ordered a tractor from Chicago. By the time his order arrived, the price of coffee had reached its lowest point on the world market. My grandfather and Petit-Goâve had gone bankrupt, they lost everything. Fortunately, the people in Chicago continued sending him their monthly catalogue. The first pictures I saw were photographs of tractors on the plains of the United States. They showed farmers working in giant fields of wheat on tractors painted yellow, Aunt Renée's color.

BREAD

When the catalogue arrived at the beginning of the month, my father would ease it out of its big yellow envelope and send me across the way, to Mozart's store, to buy a loaf of bread. I had to put the bread in the envelope. It would last all month. So it went, every morning, as we waited for the next catalogue that would come from Chicago with a new envelope. Our bread bags came from Chicago, Illinois! For some reason, right after my grandfather died, Chicago suddenly stopped sending us its catalogues.

THE BIG ROOM

It's the biggest room in the house, after the old storage and coffee-sorting room. Da's, my mother's, my five aunts' room. My grandfather has never set foot in it. My narrow bed is stuck between two large armoires. Across from mine is a big bed where my grandmother, my mother and Aunt Renée sleep. Aunt Renée always takes the very edge of the bed, a hair's breadth from falling off. As stiff as a poker, Aunt Renée never moves an inch. She never gets up during the night. Her chamber-pot is always clean. Da says you could drink warm milk out of it.

THE QUEENS

Aunt Raymonde has a little bed made of mahogany, which she shares with Aunt Ninine. It was a gift from Hiram, Da's brother. The large armoire belongs to Da—in other words, to everyone. The smaller one belongs to the older sisters: my mother and Aunt Raymonde. Aunt Renée, Aunt Ninine and Aunt Gilberte hang their dresses wherever they can. The five sisters wear the same clothes. Except for Aunt Gilberte, who is too small. When there is a dance in town, it looks as if a hurricane has blown through. Especially if everyone wants to wear the same dress. The smells of perfume mingle together, hats get passed from hand to hand, shoes go flying overhead. Everyone is late. The fateful hour strikes. The five queens—the queen of sugar, salt, sisal, flour and coffee—emerge from the room that they have left as devastated as a battlefield. Silence reigns. Da and I stay behind in the room. We say a prayer before we go to sleep.

THE DINING ROOM

Da's domain. Da has always fed everyone. Her family, the neighbors, even indigents who come by at an opportune time. Not to mention the dogs that Marquis invites. That makes a lot of bowls, white for the family, blue for the others.

Da has never forgotten anyone, except Aunt Gilberte. No one knows why. Which means she always ends up giving her bowl to Aunt Gilberte. I've never seen Da eat. When everyone is finished, she makes herself a cup of coffee and goes out under the mango tree to enjoy it.

THE LAST MEAL

Once a month, my grandfather would go to inspect his land, by the cemetery, across from Duvivier's old still. He would spend the day there and not come back until late in the evening. His lunch waited for him under a pink plastic cover, in the dining room. A few flies buzzed around the dishes, just on principle. His favorite meal: plantain, chayote, aubergine, a bit of rice (cooked without salt), with pigeon peas in a sauce. No meat, no carrots. Da always says that my grandfather and children are the only ones who don't like carrots. He would sit, eat slowly, and always cut himself a slice of pineapple for dessert. After his meal, my grandfather would clean his teeth at great length. They were his pride. He kept all his teeth till the very end.

One evening, he seemed more tired than usual. He hardly touched his dinner, brushed his teeth for a long time, then went to bed. One final time.

DEATH

We found him the next morning, in his bed, stiff and cold.
"What is death, Da?"
"You'll see."

A MAN FROM LES PALMES

I didn't see anything because they wouldn't let me in the

room. People came and left. Men, mostly. My grandfather was a Freemason. Men with black armbands whom I'd never seen before. Women I didn't know, weeping and raising their arms to the sky. A man came down from Les Palmes when he heard the news. He must have pushed his horse to the limit, leaving it half-dead in the yard, then he strode into my grandfather's room. The people there went out so he could be alone with my grandfather. He stayed there an hour, then came out. He shook Da's hand. He jumped back on his horse and galloped away.

NAILS

I went into the big room. I pushed aside the statue of the Virgin on the little table, where there's a hole in the wall. I pressed my right eye to the hole. And saw nothing. Only his feet and his clean nails. They had tied his two big toes together with a yellow ribbon. Like the ones our sacks of coffee wear.

Da says our fingernails continue to grow, even after we die. I spent a long time looking at my grandfather's nails.

THE RED ROSE

My mother and my aunts went into the yard and cut all the roses to make a giant bouquet. Da came to get me to go in and see my grandfather. He was dressed in his blue serge suit he would wear once a year to meet Bombace. The roses were all around him. A heavy, stifling smell. My grandfather was wearing his patent leather shoes and a tie with tongues of fire on it. Aunt Renée had slipped a red rose between his fingers.

5. THE DOG

Da gently put her coffee pot by the leg of her chair. A solid Jacmel chair. When someone tells you it's a Jacmel chair, that means something.

"What does it mean, Da?"

"They're the best chairs."

"Is Jacmel far?"

"Do you see that dark cloud?"

"Yes."

"It's over Jacmel."

"So this chair comes from a long way away."

"From a very long way."

Da settles comfortably in her chair to watch the people go by.

I AM AN EEL

I hate sitting down. I prefer the horizontal position. That's why my spine is as soft as an eel. I'd like to be an eel and go sliding through the river. No legs, no arms, no bottom.

"I know a little boy," says Da, "who'd like to be an eel. But I don't know any eels who'd like to be a little boy."

Da really talks well. Somewhere, there must be an eel who'd like to sit on a Jacmel chair. An eel on a chair—now, that means something.

"What does it mean?" Da asks me.

"It means that there's an eel who got tricked by a little boy."

Da tells the eel story to everyone who stops to chat with her.

THE JOURNEY

Under the terrible midday sun, the street is empty. Not a living soul, as Da says. In the distance, near the National Boys School, I see Marquis coming up the little slope. He looks out of breath. A skinny dog walking, dragging his back feet. He throws his rear end sharply to the left; that's how he moves forward. Marquis had a bad accident five years ago. He had fallen asleep in the middle of a tuft of grass, on the side of the street, when the black car arrived. Without a sound. Its front wheel ran over his back. Its left rear wheel did too. Without a sound, Marquis dragged himself to the little cemetery. He was able to slip through the tall grass behind Duvivier's still. After that, he disappeared. We looked for him everywhere, we looked as far as Miragoâne. No one could catch him. From time to time, someone claimed he'd spotted him somewhere.

PRAYER

Every evening, I pray to the Infant Jesus of Prague to bring me back Marquis, safe and sound. I also pray to Our Lady and Saint Jude, the patron saint of hopeless causes. I've stopped eating supper since Marquis disappeared. Every night, I see him in my dreams, running. We all try to catch him, but he slips through our fingers. Sometimes, he's as small as a toy. Other times, he looks like a famished wolf. Often, I wake up at night with a start and call Marquis with all my might. Da takes me into her bed.

THE RETURN

A man from Les Palmes, who used to sell coffee to my grandfather, said he'd come across Marquis near Zabo, in the cold lands. We looked everywhere in the area. Hiram, Da's brother who lives in Zabo, searched for him too. As far as Bainet. No sign of Marquis. We had lost all hope when, one morning, he jumped up on my bed and lay down in his favorite position. His stomach on my legs. Something soft and warm, a feeling I love. No one heard him enter. All the doors were locked. Da said that, to come all the way from Zabo, he must have walked a good two weeks. In his state, it must have taken him twice the time.

HUNTING CRAYFISH

If you go out the back door of the house, you step right onto the rue Desvignes. The river is there, at the end of the street. A shady, slightly humid street. You can hear the river even before you reach Germain's gaming house. I've fished in that river before. You use a reed basket to catch crayfish. You go up the river slowly, paying special attention to the edges. When you see their antennae move, you push the basket down to the bottom and lift it up quickly over your head. Once an eel wrapped itself around my ankle. The water was like glass. The eel was a silver bracelet.

THE DEVIEUX HOUSE

The black car, the one that ran over Marquis, belongs to Devieux, the richest man in the town. He lives at the end of the rue Desvignes, near the river. We used to steal mangos from Devieux all the time. We jumped over the old wall. The brightly lit house at the back, behind the coconut trees.

A big white house. All you had to do was reach down and pick up the mangos. As soon as the dogs started barking, you ran like the wind and jumped over the wall again. Marquis held his ground for a few seconds and barked too, just for show. Then he scaled the wall and started running as if he'd seen the devil himself. The devil was an enormous German shepherd that ate a quarter of beef every day.

That's how you can tell rich people, Da says. They leave fruit to rot on the ground.

THE BLACK CAR

The black car goes past our gallery every day at noon. Da knows the young man who drives the car. She helped him get into the National Boys School. His mother came and thanked Da with melons from her garden. Every time the young chauffeur comes by, he slows down a bit and nods to Da. He wasn't driving when the car ran over Marquis. The other chauffeur, the old one, was at the wheel. He isn't from Petit-Goâve. Marquis always knows who is driving the car. When it's the old man, Marquis won't stop barking until the car has disappeared past the Croix de la Jubilée. When it's the young one, he raises his head nonchalantly and watches the car go by through half-closed eyes.

WHAT TIME IS IT?

The young chauffeur always manages to drive by our gallery at exactly twelve noon. As soon as he does, Da goes into the house to make fresh coffee. Zette always comes out just then to ask what time it is. Zette lives across from us, to the left of Mozart's shop.

"What time is it, Da?"

"The Devieux car just went by, so it must be noon."

"So that means, an hour ago, it was eleven o'clock."
"I wouldn't swear to it!"
"Thanks anyway, Da."
Zette snaps her door shut. Da and I can't help laughing.

MARQUIS

He's lying next to me, as sad as can be. His nose is wet, his eyes, half-closed. Two or three flies circle above his head. Marquis tries to shoo them with his paw, but without much conviction. I rest my feet on his warm stomach without hurting him. He opens one eye to look at me, then goes back to sleep. But all it takes is another dog going by in the street for him to wake up and start barking like mad.

6. RAIN

JACMEL RAIN

A fine, slanting rain. The golden color of afternoon. Old Aurélia from the rue Geffrard comes back from vespers, holding little Clara's hand tightly. Big black clouds loom from behind the old mountain.

"This rain comes from Jacmel," Da says.

"How do you know?"

"Jacmel rains come quickly."

The rain is upon us already, strong and violent. The old woman pulls on the girl's hand; her feet scarcely touch the ground. Slowly, they disappear, as behind a curtain.

THE SOUND OF THE RAIN

The sound of rain comes from afar: a kind of rumbling. Suddenly, the clear sky turns dark. The rain is on its way. Zette gathers her washing quickly. The low rumbling grows nearer. Da looks happy.

THE TASTE OF EARTH

This mad desire to devour the earth during a rain—where does it come from? From its very smell, no doubt. At first, the earth is mute. Then, when the rain begins to fall, the smells rise up. The smell of earth. Mango smells like mango. Pineapple smells like pineapple. Sweetsop smells like nothing else than sweetsop. The earth smells of the earth.

LITTLE SPIDERS

Little spiders with delicate legs appear from the holes the rain has dug. Little by little, they take over the gallery. The ants' territory. The little blue spiders are cute. Like babies. They'll be devoured by the ferocious, underhanded, sly old ants. A fight to the death.

THE NOTARY

A man is walking in the rain. The notary. He's dressed in white, with cane and hat. All around him, people are running every which way. Like flying ants.

Loné the notary, of the rue Desvignes, believes that a man worthy of the name never runs to get out of the rain.

BOYS

The smell of manure rises in the rain. Wet manure. The game continues all the same. I hear them shouting. The ball goes flying across the street and rolls into Mozart's shop. Bare-chested, Auguste runs after the ball that bounces among the sacks of sugar. Mozart tries to catch the ball in the air. Auguste is quicker than he is. Now Mozart wants to take Auguste prisoner in his shop. The others show up and surround Mozart and Auguste. Mozart lets go of Auguste's arm. Triumphant shouts. They sprint back to the park.

DOCTOR CAYEMITTE

Doctor Cayemitte came by this morning. He told Da I was still too weak. I pretended I was asleep during their conversation. Da told him that you can't keep a young colt from running. Doctor Cayemitte asked that I be given beef liver with watercress and plenty of milk. He prescribed a syrup that I'm to take three times a day. If all goes well, he added, I'll be able to leave the room in two weeks.

"Two weeks! That's much too long, Doctor."

The doctor turned to me and smiled.

"So you weren't sleeping, you young whipper-snapper."

"He hears everything," Da said. "You can't say anything when he's around, especially if he's sleeping."

THE BORDER

The rain abates, then comes down twice as hard. The wind pushes it toward Zette's gallery. The sharp, dry click of rain on yellow bricks. The passers-by who took shelter there have to squeeze together. The rain is gaining ground. The group of people becomes more compact. The wet part of the gallery ends where the dry part begins. Like black and white. As if someone had drawn a border.

CLEAR SKIES

Suddenly the rain stops. The sky becomes clearer, the sun, warmer. Life continues as it was. The people laugh as they leave Zette's gallery. I've noticed that after a hard but brief downpour, people seem happier.

WET DOG

Marquis comes onto the gallery. Completely soaked. He had followed Naréus' ducks in the rain. Now his fur is stuck to his body. Marquis gives me a guilty look, then shakes himself off vigorously. Water goes flying everywhere: in my face, on Da's dress. I chase him into the street. He gives me an even sadder look. I hold my ground. He shakes himself off in the street, then comes back onto the gallery and lies down by the scale.

VAVA'S MOTHER

Da gives me a searching look. She does that when she wants to send me a signal. Someone is coming up behind me. I don't know who. I won't turn around. I feel a living thing behind me. From the corner of my left eye I see two shadows. Vava and her mother. Vava, always wearing yellow. Her eyes, my God, Vava's eyes! Those eyes that keep me awake at night. Vava's mother greets Da.

"How are you, Da?"

"Fine, Délia."

Vava's mother is named Délia. Da says she was exactly like her daughter. Da knew her when she was Vava's age.

"Would you care for a cup of coffee, Délia?"

"No, thank you. I have to be running along. I have to make a dress for Vava. She's going to wear it tomorrow, for Nissage's party."

I don't know what made me say, "A yellow dress."

Vava's mother looked at me and smiled.

"Yes," she said. "A yellow dress."

We were all silent for a moment.

"Well," said Vava's mother, "I'd better be going."

"Will you come for coffee another time, Délia?"

"Of course, Da."

I watch them go as they walk to the Croix de la Jubilée. There, they take the road to the left that runs past the town reservoir.

DUCKS

Naréus' ducks are returning home. They walk down the street in single file. The ducklings stop at every puddle the rain has left. They thrust their heads into the water, then pop up a second or two later. The ducklings seem to be in a constant state of astonishment. The older ducks herd them together, quacking loudly. The ducklings follow them, but only for a step or two, then they go back to their puddles.

LIGHT

Sunshine always seems brighter after a rain. As if each puddle has captured a sunbeam. A glow in the heart of the water. The eyes of the earth.

THE CROWD

Suddenly, people appear from everywhere. Everyone who had taken shelter, waiting for the rain to stop, now pours into the street. Life has recovered its color.

MAN IN A HURRY

A man goes by, running behind his mule, and calls out to Da without taking the time to stop.

"I have something to tell you, Da, but I'm in a hurry, I have to see Jérôme before the sun goes down."

"Later, Absalom ... I'm always here."

THE OLD WOMAN

Old Cornélia is going to buy her tobacco at Mozart's shop. Her legs are so frail she has to walk on her rear end. Zette opens her windows. Thérèse forgot to bring in her laundry before it started raining. Now she hopes the sun will stay out long enough to dry it before sunset.

That's the way Jacmel rain is: hard but short-lived.

7. PEOPLE

THE RED DEVIL

I've always been afraid of Brother Jérôme. He plays the devil every year, for Carnival. He has long, pointy fingernails. Great black wings and webbed feet. A long tail hangs from his rear end. For the three days before Ash Wednesday, Brother Jérôme really is the devil. His eyes are red and his mouth spits fire. After Carnival, Brother Jérôme goes back to being the most gentle shoeshine man in the world. Every day, he moves down the street, shining everyone's shoes. Those who can pay him do so; it's free for those who can't. On Monday, he does the rue Dessalines. Tuesday is the rue Geffrard's turn. He goes down to Petite Guinée on Wednesdays. On Thursday, to La Hatte. He covers the rue Fraternité on Friday. Saturday is a good day because he does the Lodge. All the important men in town can be found there. The Freemasons are known for their shiny shoes. Brother Jérôme doesn't have to work too hard to pocket a pretty penny at the Lodge. He does our street on Saturday too, and spends Sunday at La Plaine, at his sister's house. Brother Jérôme is Da's faithful informant. Thanks to him, Da knows everything that is happening in town, without ever having to leave her old Jacmel chair.

THE TRUCK

Big Simon's truck just came flying around the corner with

no warning and almost hit Brother Jérôme, who was coming out of the courthouse. Big Simon burst out laughing as if it were an enormous joke, as Brother Jérôme jumped into the little gully by the National Boys School. Big Simon was still laughing when he reached Da's gallery. Marquis, who was lying by the scale, showed his fangs. Marquis doesn't like drivers too much, ever since his accident. Da didn't say anything. She didn't want Big Simon to bring up the business of the roof again. He'll probably say he was blinded by Da's new roof. That's why Da avoided him. Da has a foolproof technique for ignoring people. She pretends she's filling her cup just as they go past her. I've noticed she does that with certain people whose names I won't mention.

DEATH

I don't know if it's because of my fever, but I can't stop thinking about death.
     "Why do we die, Da?"
     "Why do we sleep?"
     "To rest."
     "So?"
     "So what, Da?"
     "Death is eternal rest."

BIG SIMON'S VERSION

Before becoming the fortunate owner of this new truck, the pride of all Petit-Goâve, Big Simon was an ordinary longshoreman, though the strongest one. He worked for the Maison Bombace. Big Simon said that, one night, he had a dream. In his dream, his old grandmother Sylphise, who's been dead for years, asked him to get up and go outside. Big Simon got up and went out in his pajamas. He walked down the rue Fraternité, turned onto the rue La-Paix and went as far as the wayside cross. He sat down on the steps there, waiting for who-knows-what, until Simplicius came along with his swaying gait. He bought a strip of lottery tickets from Simplicius. The next day, he won the grand prize. That's Big Simon's version.

BROTHER JÉRÔME'S VERSION

According to Brother Jérôme, it didn't happen the way Big Simon told it. The truth was much more terrible. Big Simon sold his only daughter to the devil, poor, sweet-natured Sylphise who bears the name of her great-grandmother. Brother Jérôme heard the story at the Freemasons' Lodge where Big Simon goes. The transaction was made on Soldier Mountain, in Wilberforce the priest's yard, in his temple. A few days later, on Monday noon, Big Simon won the grand prize in the lottery and became richer than Croesus. "I know Big Simon will deny it, but if it's not true, why did his daughter die at exactly the same time? Mystery? Coincidence? Da, you and I know that life is not that simple … The affairs of men are very complex … Every time I see Big Simon, I wonder how a man could give his daughter to the devil in exchange for worldly goods … Ah, Da, let me go now, I've said too much already."

ANTS

"What happens after you die, Da?"
      "Only the ants can answer that."
      "Why don't they tell us?"
      "Because death doesn't interest them, Old Bones."
      "And why does death interest us?"

"Because it's the key to life."

OGINÉ'S VERSION

According to Oginé, the old man who takes care of the park, Brother Jérôme's version is not completely correct. True, Big Simon did contact Wilberforce the priest, but he refused the bargain, saying he wasn't a two-handed priest, which means he wouldn't serve two masters. He wouldn't do good with his right hand and evil with his left. "You understand, Da, what I'm getting at. Wilberforce, the way I know him, would never agree to take the life of an innocent girl. When Wilberforce refused, Big Simon went to see Gervilien, the evil priest of Marinette Mountain. He made the transaction on a Thursday evening, in the little cemetery, near the spring. I don't want people to say it was Wilberforce, Da. He's my cousin and he doesn't do evil."

MOZART'S VERSION

The little girl isn't dead, Da. I saw her with my own eyes, in Miragoâne, at Reyer's house, the white man who's been living there for thirty years. He claims he's studying Haitian culture, but the fellow is the devil himself. He didn't learn evil in our country. We didn't write the book on evil, I'm telling you. This Reyer is a German, and Germans know a thing or two about the subject. Haitians always think they're the best in everything, including evil. Anyway, I was at Reyer's house, I was thirsty and Reyer gave me a glass of grenadine. And guess who came in to serve me, Da? Right, it was little Sylphise herself. I pretended not to recognize her. I took the juice and drank it to the last drop. I had business on the waterfront. I picked up my hat and said goodbye to

Reyer. That's how it happened. Reyer scarcely said a word when I was there. Neither did the girl. She kept her eyes lowered the entire time. A zombie, that's what I saw. The more I think about it, the more I think Big Simon sold her to Reyer. Reyer may well be a German devil, and that's the worst kind, believe me, Da, but still, he'd never make a zombie out of Big Simon's daughter. If you ask me, Big Simon made the bargain himself.

ZETTE'S VERSION

If there's one person you have to keep your eye on, Da, it's that little toad Mozart with his green lizard head. He already tried twice with my sister Thérèse's daughter. I told him he was a sorry little devil and that if he didn't watch out, I'd eat him alive, myself. I wouldn't be surprised if he was involved with that business with Big Simon's daughter. All he cares about is whether his name was mentioned. That's all, Da. Nothing more.

DOCTOR CAYEMITTE'S VERSION

I was the girl's physician, Da, for the last three years. She suffered from extremely severe headaches. I sent her to Port-au-Prince for every test imaginable; they found nothing. She was taking all manner of medicines to fight her migraine, but it was never enough. She had terrible nosebleeds when her migraine struck. What could I do, when even the laboratories in Port-au-Prince were unable to isolate the disease? What I'm saying, Da, is that I could do nothing to fight her illness, but contrary to what people say—which is that she died without ever having been sick—she was very ill. More than people think. Much more. What did she have? No one knows. I asked for an autopsy, but the family refused. My hands were tied. Had I had better instruments, we might have stopped the disease from progressing. But, then again, what disease? Sometimes, Da, we feel so helpless that we just want to sit down and drink till we pass out. What defense do we have against the unknown? When a disease will not speak its name, Da, we can't call it out. There's nothing we can do. Just wait for it to take its course. Honestly, I was surprised, I never thought the end would come so quickly. That's what life is, Da. Nothingness.

SIMPLICIUS' VERSION

It's true, Da, Big Simon was sitting on the steps of the wayside cross that night when I turned onto the rue La-Paix. He saw me, came toward me and bought all the tickets I had. I've been selling lottery tickets here in Petit-Goâve for twenty years, and that's the first time it happened. Big Simon was in pajamas and it looked like he'd just gotten out of bed. But it was more than that. He looked bewildered, as if he had lost his reason, as if someone else were manipulating him. I know Big Simon, I've known him for years, and I've never seen him like that. The way he was that night. He looked as if he'd been drinking, but he didn't smell of alcohol. It was a strange night, Da. When I got home, my wife said I seemed odd to her. I told her what had happened with Big Simon. "So what?" she asked me. He looked strange and he bought all my tickets. I went to bed and the next day, around noon, when I found out that Big Simon had won the grand prize, I was only half-surprised. My wife, whom nothing impresses, was more astonished than I was. People said there was blood on his right hand when he paid for the tickets, but that's just talk. I even heard he had cloven hooves on his feet. I was alone in the street with him that night, and I never saw anything like that. That's all I have to say, Da.

ZINA'S VERSION

Sylphise and I were always together, in school and out. We were always in the same class, on the same bench. Even Sister Noel couldn't separate us. At recess, we were always under the big sandbox tree, near the canteen. Sylphise was my best friend. I was with her the day she died. It was a Monday. She said she had a headache. I didn't pay much attention because she always had one. And, I have to admit, Sylphise didn't much like doing homework, and on Mondays we had a lot of homework to turn in. I said to myself, Sylphise is looking for an excuse not to turn in her homework. Sister Noel is very strict about it. All morning, she kept her head down, as if her neck couldn't hold the weight any more. That worried me a little, but not too much because, like I said, she had terrible headaches that never left her a moment's peace. At eleven o'clock we left the classroom. I helped her get home. At her house, there wasn't anything to eat. Her mother hadn't come back. Luckily, she wasn't hungry. She never ate when she had a headache. She lay down on her mother's bed, sideways. I took off her shoes and pushed her legs toward the middle of the bed. I decided to leave and go back home, because once she gets some rest, her headache disappears. She called out and asked me to bring her a glass of salt water; she must have wanted to make a compress. I went to get the water, and as I was coming back, I heard a terrible noise in the room. As if a horrible struggle was taking place. It sounded like there were several people in the room. Sylphise was shouting that she wanted to be left alone, that she didn't want to go. She screamed, "Don't touch me ... I don't know you." I went into the room and saw her body floating in the air, ten centimeters off the bed. She fell back on the bed when I screamed. The last word she said was "No!"

AUGEREAU'S VERSION

Before, I was at the Maison Devieux, and I had a little falling-out with the director, a man named Montal. I was sorry to leave Devieux because they had been good bosses. I went to work at Customs and had a fight with Willy Bony, my best friend, who had become Customs director in the meantime. To save our friendship, I left and went to work with Céphas at the Maison Bombace. At the time, Céphas was getting together a good team to try to put the Maison Bombace, which had been wandering in the desert, back on its feet. Céphas made me chief of the longshoreman service. Solid guys who could work twelve hours straight without running out of steam. That's where I met Big Simon, our best longshoreman. He was worth three solid stevedores himself. A born leader, too. Some people were jealous of him, they said he wasn't working alone. You understand, Da, they thought he was invested with powerful spirits that helped him carry the sacks of coffee. He had a strong back; he didn't know what tired meant. As for the truck, Big Simon had been planning it, he'd been telling me for as long as I can remember that he was trying to put money aside to buy himself a diesel truck. He dreamed of setting up a route between Port-au-Prince and Petit-Goâve. He would drive passengers, merchandise and even the surplus coffee that the boat couldn't take to the capital. He'd been dreaming of that for ten years. When I heard he'd won the grand prize, I said to myself, Now Big Simon will be able to buy his truck. As for the death of little Sylphise, that was only an unfortunate coincidence.

LONÉ THE NOTARY'S VERSION

The entire business was concocted by jealous minds. That wasn't the first time a child died in our misbegotten country, and it won't be the last. Every time it's the same story. It wasn't death from natural causes. I tell them death is never natural, that it has causes that can be scientifically analyzed. But the workings of the mind are not for them. Jealousy, back-stabbing, envy—that's what they feed on. Nothing in their heads; everything in their guts. Our society is full of shit, Da. Excuse my language, but that's the best way to describe it. I don't know this Simon, nor his truck, nor his poor little girl, but therein lie all the elements of a Haitian tragedy. Da, I've been observing this society for a long time now, and what do I see? The same thing. Sound and fury, signifying nothing. Nothing has changed, and nothing ever will.

ZETTE'S NEW VERSION

Da, beware of Loné the notary, for his name has been mentioned too. It seems he has an acquaintanceship with Gervilien the priest. In any case, you can't trust a man who walks in the rain without getting wet. Not a single drop touches him, Da.

ABSALOM'S VERSION

I live near the iron bridge, not far from the little cemetery. The children's cemetery. I live practically right across from it. The land belongs to Lavertu, the surveyor. He bought it from Duvivier and gave me permission to build a little house on one part of it. I planted a few mango and banana trees too. I live alone, ever since Saintanise, my late spouse, died. She's buried in the big cemetery, near your cousin Hannibal. I've

been living on this lot for nearly forty years now, and I'm
seventy years old and counting. I know the area like the back
of my hand. I know every gravestone, Da. I clean some of
them myself. Da, there are respectable people in this town
who don't look after their dead. As far as I'm concerned, and
I'll say it out loud, they aren't human beings, they're just
mounds of flesh. Da, if you really want to know what people
are like, observe how they treat their dead. I won't mention
any names, Da, but you'd be amazed to know what I know.
I often spend my time in the cemetery, and I find myself
talking to the people there. I was born in this town. I know
everyone, and many are those who live in the cemetery now.
Good and bad alike. As my late mother used to say, there are
good masks and bad. Because we all wear a mask, Da. Some
people respect others, and some think they're above the rest
of us mortals. Some think the world revolves around them.
I'll tell you something, Da, they're all beneath my feet now.
Not that I intend any disrespect, but that's reality, the only
reality there is. The worms will feast on me too, one day.
That day might not be far off. But the only injustice is when
the children go first. I'm an old dog and it's too late for any
new tricks. But there was no reason little Sylphise had to go
so soon. I haven't stopped thinking about it, ever since that
night, the night of her funeral. It was very warm, I remember. I went out and lit my pipe on Dorméus' grave, the one
closest to my house. Dorméus was a good friend of mine
when he was alive. I was so lost in my thoughts, watching the
stars, that I didn't see them coming. There were a half dozen
of them. With ashes smeared on their bodies. They were
dancing naked around the little girl's freshly dug grave. I
supposed they were going to dig her up, so I didn't stay to
watch the whole ceremony. A man who lives by the cemetery and wants to stay alive learns to keep his nose out of

other people's business. Still, I don't think it's fair. The little girl never hurt anyone. How can you harm an angel, Da?

OGINÉ'S NEW VERSION

I hope no one's listening, Da, but I have to tell you the truth. I didn't tell you everything the other day. It's true that my cousin Wilberforce, the priest, was never involved in that business with Big Simon's daughter. But I'm the one who suggested to Big Simon to go see Gervilien, the priest of Marinette Mountain. I even took him there. I did it because I'm in debt to Gervilien, and my date had come due. It was for my son's cure. I was in a tight spot, I didn't know what to do. If I didn't pay, Gervilien would take back my son's life. It's true that I took Big Simon to see Wilberforce first. Wilberforce told him that he didn't do good with the right hand and evil with the left. So I asked Big Simon if he was ready to go see Gervilien. He turned pale. He asked for three days to think about it. Big Simon knows that once you've seen Gervilien, you can't go back. Finally, we set a time and went out there. We left in the afternoon, and by ten o'clock in the evening, we could see Gervilien's temple in the distance. We weren't the only ones there. Da, if I told you the names of the people waiting to see Gervilien, you'd fall off your chair. I saw the most important people in the town there. We waited, and finally Philo came to get us. I walked with Big Simon to the temple door, but he went inside alone. When he finally came out, his face was white. We walked all night without saying a word. Near Petite Guinée, we met a group of men who stopped us. Gervilien had given Big Simon a pass. He showed it to the leader. I knew who they were: Dieudonné's men. Raging demons. They would eat you where you stood and not even tell you why. I embraced

Dieudonné. They told me they were going to get Yaya, the fat lady from Vialet who lives behind the church. I left Big Simon at his house and went to the market to get some sleep and wait for the horses that start coming in around five o'clock in the morning. The little girl died two days later, a Monday noon, and Big Simon won the grand prize. Gervilien asked me to take five trustworthy men with me to get the child, the very night she was buried. I took Augereau, Loné the notary, Zette, Brother Jérôme and Mozart. We did what we had to and everything was fine. I know that Absalom saw us, but he never sticks his nose into other people's business. Da, I know you're wondering how it is that I would give orders to Augereau and Loné the notary, I, a man who looks after an empty lot. The night is different from the day. At night, the country gets turned upside down. Everything that was on top descends, and everything that was at the bottom rises. I'm not telling you anything you don't already know, Da.

PART II

8. BODIES

It likes to do it in the afternoon. Suddenly, for no reason, in the middle of a meal, or talking with Da, or simply studying my geography lesson, or even running across to Mozart's shop to do an errand. Suddenly, my heart starts beating at top speed. I feel it will jump out of my chest and land on the ground. I can see it there at my feet, all dirty and about to be devoured by a colony of flying ants. When that happens, I have to stop all movement, for she isn't far. Vava is in the neighborhood. I feel her coming closer. My stomach begins to churn. My head is empty. I'm running with sweat. My hands are wet. I feel sick. I'm going to die.

THE CORAL TREES

Early in June, the coral trees in the schoolyard of the Brothers of Christian Instruction start to flower. The end-of-term examinations are about to begin. I've stopped sleeping because I'm afraid that Vava will go to her aunt's house in Port-au-Prince once classes are over. I can't eat a thing. I pretend to, and manage to fool Da. In any case, Da's only nourishment is the coffee of Les Palmes. I'm starting to get really thin. I who was already skinny. Da says she's noticed that I waste away every time the coral trees begin to flower.

DIET

Da puts me on a diet: curdled milk, watercress, beef tongue, pig's blood, carrot and aubergine. I hate it. I hate everything that's good for me. Carrots are good for your eyes. I hate carrots. Da makes me eat, otherwise, it's cod-liver oil every day. To clean my blood.

A REED

Despite the intensive diet, I'm still as thin as a reed. I'm so thin the teacher can't find a place fleshy enough—not even my bottom—to cane me. I know how to play the game. I have two kinds of pants for school. When I know my lessons, I wear a pair that makes me look huskier. When I haven't done my homework, I put on another pair that makes me look as though I'm going to drop dead of starvation at any minute. The teacher doesn't dare lay a hand on me. But my body doesn't help me much with girls.

CRACKERS

Philomena, Doctor Cayemitte's daughter, invited me to the baptism of her doll. I brought a box of Ritz crackers. Everyone brought the same thing, which meant we spent the evening eating crackers. Everyone danced. I didn't budge from my seat. Philomena came over and danced with me once. Then I didn't see her again. Didi would have danced with me if I'd wanted to, but I'm too old to dance with my girl cousins. Frantz came up and told me that a girl wanted to dance with me.

"Where is she?"

"Over there."

"Over where, Frantz?"

"Do you want me to go and get her?" he said ironically. "All right, all right ... I'll come."

I went into the next room with Frantz. The girl was his cousin. She's really ugly. I knew it. Frantz pushed me and I fell on top of her. What a fool he is. I told her I was sorry and went back to my seat. There were still some crackers left.

ELECTRIC WIRE

Auguste says I'm so thin that if it rains, I can take shelter under an electric wire. But I'm not afraid of fighting. I use my feet, my teeth. The other day, a kid from the rue Fraternité pointed to me and said, "There goes the girl."

I nearly ripped off his left ear.

A BLINDMAN

Just past the rue Dessalines is a big vacant lot where we go to fight after school. I have a trick that always works: I fill my schoolbag with stones, close my eyes, and wale away like a blindman. Every time I hear a thud, I know I've hit one. I open my eyes when it's over. There's no one left on the field.

MY SHADOW

In the afternoon, when we come back from school, we compare our shadows. Mine is always the longest, as if I were a skinny giant.

COMFORT

My grandfather died in April, in the middle of spring, he who loved flowers so much. My mother went to join my father in Port-au-Prince. My aunts went soon after. Sometimes, Da and I try to imagine what they're doing there. Da has never been to Port-au-Prince. I went once, but my experience doesn't count for much. My mother and my aunts send long letters to Da. I read them because Da has bad eyes. Sometimes, when there are no new letters, we sit on the gallery and read old letters from two or three months ago.

Da says I am her comfort in her old age.

9. SEX

THE WALL

Auguste convinced me to do it. Just climb a wall, and you're in Ismela's garden. Then you go over a second wall and drop into the National Boys School yard. No one is there on Saturdays. There's always a door open. The classrooms are very dim. Auguste leads me by the hand. We walk on our tiptoes, as if we were going to steal pineapples from Passilus' patch. Auguste knows the place, he goes to school there. I go to the Brothers of Christian Instruction. The Brothers live in the school. And they never get sick. The National School is freer. Da will never send me to a school where the students hardly have any homework. Auguste says his mother likes it better that way. She couldn't help him anyway. She doesn't know how to read or write. His mother comes from the sixth rural section, not far from Abraham's land. She came to Petit-Goâve to look after Auguste. He can make her believe anything. She has him recite his lessons in the morning. He gives her the book to hold and recites a lesson from three days ago. Auguste tells her he's at the head of the class, while actually, he's bringing up the rear. Sometimes, his mother gets suspicious and, for no good reason, slaps him so hard he sees stars. The neighbors get involved. And they discover that, this time, for once, Auguste didn't lie. Out of remorse, his mother babies him for the next month.

INK

Auguste takes me to his classroom. He sits down on his bench. I play the fool in front of the desk as if I were the teacher. He pretends he's reciting his lessons, but can't find the words. His face is a mask of convulsions. He leaps from his seat and rushes the teacher's desk. He throws me on the ground and tramples me. We're sweating bullets. We fight for a while in the soft shadow. As abruptly as he started the fight, Auguste jumps up and gets undressed. He strips completely naked. I get undressed too. Each of us lie on a desk and stick our penises in the little inkwells. Long desks where a dozen students can sit side by side, and every student has an inkwell. Auguste looks as if he's in pain. I make the same face he does. Auguste makes a worse face. He starts making a whistling noise with his mouth. He asks me if it's coming. I say yes because I've been wanting to piss for a while now. Auguste says, "If it comes, let yourself go." I start pissing. Auguste looks at me incredulously, then jumps on me. The piss and ink mixture makes a blue puddle. Auguste punches me in the back. I can't stop pissing. When I start pissing, nothing can stop me. Auguste tells me that's how you do it with girls. Their sex: a black hole with liquid inside. Midnight blue.

HORSE

I am sitting on the gallery, almost at the end, where it meets the house. I saw Oginé's little trick. He moved Naréus' horse and put it next to Chaël Charles' mare. Two well-behaved animals. Suddenly, the horse started whinnying and pulling on its rope. Its penis was as stiff as a broomstick. Big Simon's truck went by just then, raising a little dust.

Marquis, lying by the scale, woke up with a start and started barking. The truck had reached the Croix de la Jubilée when the horse broke through the rope and jumped the mare. That's when Da sent me inside to get her coffee pot.

ANGER

Naréus came walking up the street, talking to himself. The black automobile glided past him, nearly touching him. Naréus raised his fist to the sky. He went past Da.

"Naré, what's the matter?"

"Oginé's the matter, Da. I told him not to touch my horse, and he pushed him onto Chaël Charles' mare."

"That's what someone told you, Naré, but that's not what I saw."

"What did you see, Da?"

"Your horse was in heat and he broke his lead."

"If you say so, Da ... All the same, I'd better see Oginé. I warned him not to put Chaël Charles' mare in the park with my horse. If he had told me, I would have tied up the horse in my yard."

"That's what you should have done, Naré. But I'm telling you, it wasn't Oginé's fault."

Naréus shook his head. His anger had subsided. He went home to feed his ducks.

"Da," I said, "I saw Oginé move the horse."

"I did too."

"Da, how could you have seen the horse with your back to the park?"

Da poured herself a good cup of hot coffee. Time went by, and there was no one in the street. The street was white, as Da says, all the way to the sea.

THE GENDARME

A gendarme as skinny as a rail came walking down toward the barracks. He had arrested Innocent, the tailor from the rue Geffrard.

"Why do you have him handcuffed like that?" asked Da.

"Da, this man had the audacity to steal the commander's money."

"Innocent would never do something that stupid ..."

"Yes, Da, but that's what I'm saying ... He's the commander's tailor, and for two months he's refused to deliver the suit the commander paid for a long time ago."

"Da, I beg of you, try to reason with the sergeant ... The commander gave me some money to begin the job, and that's how I bought the thread and the buttons ... Every time I see the commander at the Lodge and tell him I don't have enough money to finish the job, he tells me he's still waiting for his suit, and now, he sends the sergeant after me ... Look, Da, how he's handcuffed me ... I'm a family man and an honest worker."

The sergeant looked a little shaken.

"It's not my fault, Da. The commander told me to bring in Innocent."

"Bazile, you went to school with Innocent. I remember seeing you walking past my gallery, hand in hand. You weren't even ten at the time ... Is this any way to treat a childhood friend?"

Sergeant Bazile lowered his head.

"Take those handcuffs off him and go tell the commander you couldn't find him ... And while you're at it, tell him I have a bitter cup for him."

"Yes, Da," said the sergeant.

"Thank you, Da," said Innocent.

THE INFORMER

I don't know who squealed on us. Actually, I do, it must have been Djo from the rue Pétion. He's the only one who would do that. Speak of the devil, here comes his lousy mug. Djo went into Augustine's shop. He's going to make his daily report on what Augustine's daughter Marie has been up to. He keeps an eye on her when Augustine goes to Port-au-Prince to buy flour from the wholesaler's. Djo has a head like a pin, bug-eyes and the biggest Adam's apple I've ever seen. Augustine puts her arm around Djo's shoulders. She's smiling. Djo pretends he's leaving. I know his little routine. He turns and whispers something in Augustine's ear. Augustine goes back in the shop and comes out with a sack of provisions. Djo's face lights up. Now he leaves. Out in the street, he turns and waves to Augustine one last time. Poor Marie, she's going to get her hide tanned tonight!

DA AND DJO

Da hates Djo. Once, Djo told something to Da, and she listened without a word. When he was through, he asked Da for some money for his troubles. Da didn't move a muscle. When Da has contempt for someone, she doesn't need to tell him. He knows it immediately. Djo stayed on for a while longer, talking about me, claiming he saw me on the waterfront with some hoodlums. He said I ate in the street, after school. If someone else had told her that, Da would have murdered me. But Da hates Djo so much she doesn't listen to what he says. Finally, he went away with his tail between his legs. After he left, Da asked me to avoid Djo like the plague.

BLUE

Djo was the one who squealed on us. How could he have found out? True, Auguste did introduce all our neighborhood friends to our game. A dozen of us were in Auguste's classroom when the big door flew open. We all had our pants down. We were lying on the benches when the principal caught us. He brought each of us to his office to receive the most memorable hiding of our lives. Since we all pretty much lived on the same street, he left us naked on our respective galleries so the people going by could see our blue penises.

10. ROMANTIC LOVE

THE REAL CEMETERY

Da takes the glass of water and spills some of it on the ground three times. She's paying tribute to the dead.

"The dead are in the cemetery," I tell her.

Da looks at me and smiles. For her, the dead are everywhere. Since people have been dying forever, by now there must be more dead than living on the earth.

"If there were more dead people, Da, they would have made the cemetery bigger."

"The real cemetery is everywhere. Where this house sits, once there was a tomb. When your grandfather bought this land, old Labasterre was buried here. And plenty others before him. We found a dozen gravestones."

"Da, we're living on top of a graveyard!"

"And when the town gets too small, they will make it bigger, and build new houses on top of the old stones that have fallen into dust."

Da says we're not truly dead until there's no one left on earth to remember our name.

PLAYING HOOKEY

Dieuseul came by the house to pick me up. We pretended we were going to school. Da always watches me from the gallery until I turn the corner by the courthouse. We went up the rue Dessalines to the rue Geffrard. We turned left on the rue

Desvignes and, right after Germain's gaming house, we took the narrow dirt track that leads straight to the big cemetery. Dieuseul knows the way well. Usually I cut through Lavertu the surveyor's yard and keep going straight until I see Baron Samedi's cross up ahead.

THE BARON

In the big cemetery is an empty grave with a big cross made of black wood. The tomb of Baron Samedi, the boss of the dead. Old Cornélia is always watering it, especially when the sun is at its hottest. The Baron is thirsty.

THE DEAD

Dieuseul took me to his mother's grave at the far end of the cemetery. You have to go past all the tombs. Some of them are completely ruined. Dieuseul scampers over the graves, jumping over some of them. I try to keep up, but I'm afraid of falling into a hole and ending up with a skeleton. Dieuseul runs like the wind, turning around from time to time to wave me on. At times he shows me a dangerous spot to watch out for. The grass grows over the ruined graves and if you walk on it, you might end up falling into an underground vault. Finally, we reach his mother's tomb.

DIEUSEUL'S MOTHER

According to Da, Dieuseul's mother was the most beautiful woman in all Petit-Goâve. Her lover Milord killed her one Tuesday at noon because he was jealous of her husband. Dieuseul is Milord's son. Samuel, her husband, raised Dieuseul, even before Milord's death. Milord killed himself immediately after murdering Ludna. They were buried side by side, but not in the same tomb.

THAT BLOODY DAY

Dieuseul was little when it happened. Milord, his father, came into the house with a gun. He, Dieuseul, was playing in the yard. Milord and Ludna started insulting each other, shouting for the whole town to hear. Everyone knew the routine, the same thing happened every time Samuel went to Port-au-Prince. Milord shows up and makes a scene. He wants Ludna to leave Samuel and live with him. She tells him she'll never live with a man who doesn't know what to do with himself, who isn't even capable of looking after his own son. But the legendary Milord still believes in his charm. Ludna refuses, as she does every time, to go with him. The blows begin to rain down. The neighbors are busy minding their own business. Milord threatens to blow her brains out, then turn the gun on himself. Thérèse goes on hanging out her wash on the decrepit acacia trees that form a fence around Mozart's shop. Mozart is sitting on his gallery, reading two-month-old newspapers. The noonday sun paralyzes everyone. Milord continues to beat Ludna, asking her for the thousandth time to come and live with him in his little house by the sea. Ludna answers for the thousandth time that she'll never live with a good-for-nothing. Then silence falls. Not a shout. Not a cry. Then Milord starts sobbing, begging Ludna to forgive him for the evil he's done. He begs Ludna's pardon. She's willing to forgive him, but reminds him that she'll never live with him. Everything starts all over: the insults, the blows, the tears.

THE DEATH

Thérèse remembers someone saying, "Milord is really out of

his mind today. Are we going to let him kill that poor woman?" Old Cornélia answered that it had been going on for ten years. The man went on his way, but he hadn't reached the Croix de la Jubilée when the first shot rang out. Then Milord turned the weapon on himself. He put the barrel of the gun in his mouth and fired. When the gendarmes arrived and knocked down the door, they found the two bodies one atop the other, and the gun next to them. Dieuseul didn't move from the yard where he had been playing by himself. When the body of his father was carried past, he slapped him.

THE BOUQUET

Dieuseul gathered the flowers left on other graves to make a bouquet for his mother.

11. DESTINY

In the afternoon, I like to sit with Da on the gallery. Sometimes, Da and I don't even speak until someone passes by. Odilon is urging along his donkey with an old staff full of knots. Odilon sells hay for the horses. Every afternoon around five, he goes to see Oginé who buys a bale from him. Da always greets Odilon with great ceremony.

"Do you know who that man is?"

"Yes, Da. He's the hay-seller."

"He wasn't always a hay-seller. When I was a young girl, Odilon was known as the most handsome man in Petit-Goâve. All the girls were in love with him to one extent or another."

"Even you, Da?"

"Even me. But Odilon went furthest with Ernestine. Ernestine ended up pregnant. So as not to marry her, Odilon ran away to Port-au-Prince."

"Then, overcome by remorse, he returned to marry after the child was born."

"No. He couldn't have married Ernestine because she died of shame. Ernestine's father, a man named Mabial from Les Palmes, swore that one day Odilon would return to Petit-Goâve as a beggar. A few years later, Samson went to Port-au-Prince and saw Odilon there. He'd become a regular somebody in the capital. Ernestine's father didn't move a muscle. He was sitting on the gallery when Samson told him the news. He didn't say a word. Thérèse, his wife, murmured, 'So that's how it is. He gets my daughter pregnant, then runs off to Port-au-Prince to be cock of the walk.' Mabial gritted his teeth. Thérèse started to cry and went inside the house."

"Is that all, Da?"

"The years went by and one day, Odilon returned wearing the same suit he had on when he first left Petit-Goâve. He told us he had made his fortune in bananas with the MacDonald Fruit Company, but had gone bankrupt when the company was forced into exile. He didn't have a penny and, naturally, not a single friend left. Seeing that he was going to starve to death in Port-au-Prince, he decided he'd rather die in his own home town, where he was known. By the time he reached Petit-Goâve, he was so thin no one recognized him. He was standing near the market when Thérèse spotted him for the first time since he'd come back. She jumped on him, hammering away at his chest with her little fists. The people nearby hurried to separate them. They wanted to keep Thérèse from killing this poor, defenseless devil. Thérèse was so hysterical she couldn't manage a single word. When finally she was able to speak, all she could do was murmur, 'It's Odilon ... Odilon Lauredan.' Then she fainted. The people began gathering around Odilon, and he told his story. When he finished it, they walked away in silence. Odilon started off sleeping in the market, in the fish-ladies' quarter. He smelled of fish all day long. One day, Thérèse brought him clean pants and a shirt. She washed Odilon and dressed him in front of everyone. Thérèse told him, 'My only daughter wasn't good enough for you. You humiliated her and she died of the shame. I'm not doing this for you. But my daughter (and she was crying as she spoke these words) told me on her deathbed that you were the only

man she ever loved. I won't let you sully her love this way.'
She cried all the tears there were in her body, she who had
not shed a single one the day of Ernestine's funeral. Thérèse
took him home and let him live in the little shack in the yard.
Mabial said nothing. He never mentioned the affair again.
Thérèse died a few years later. Mabial kept Odilon in his
yard without ever speaking to him. After Mabial died, his
family drove him out. Who would have thought that, one
day, I would see Odilon selling hay? Life is a mystery."

12. FEVER

THE PARTY

In the end, Da made me go to Nissage's party. I didn't want to go because I knew Vava would be there. Wearing her new yellow dress. A dress with lots of lace and a sort of train. I don't like that dress on Vava. I perspire. My body aches. I have to go home. I'm going to tell Nissage that I have to leave. The cherry punch is making my head spin. The earth leaps up at me. Nissage catches me as I fall. I end up in my bed. With Da, nearby.

THE TUNNEL

When I close my eyes hard, I see little yellow lights. There's never total darkness. Even if the room is dark.

EYES

Da says my eyes have been closed for two days. Asleep, some of the time. Other times, she thinks I was just keeping my eyes shut. Da spent the last two days calling me by my name. My real name.

MALARIA

Doctor Cayemitte visited three times in two days. He can't figure out what's the matter with me. In his opinion, I'm a little weak, which is natural, since I'm in the middle of a growth spurt. But he isn't sure. He's worried about malaria. Petit-Goâve is surrounded by swamps. Doctor Cayemitte has to leave before Friday. He'll do everything possible, he told Da, to see me before he goes. Once or twice a month, he travels to Port-au-Prince to get the results of his tests. Doctor Cayemitte had me fill a little bottle with urine, then he slipped the bottle into his jacket pocket. Da says Doctor Cayemitte is so absent-minded he could mistake the urine bottle for a vial of perfume. And use the former for scent.

THE CLINIC

That's the way Doctor Cayemitte is. He has a clinic in Vialet and, every morning, he wonders whether or not he should go there. He gets out his old bicycle, cleans the spokes with Vaseline, checks the brakes and prepares to go to his clinic. Da says that if someone happened by just then and asked him, "Doctor Cayemitte, are you going to Vialet?" he would answer in all honesty, his right foot on the pedal, "I don't know, dear woman … I'm not saying yes … But I'm not saying no either." A minute later, he'll push off hard on the pedals and turn the handlebars to the left, or to the right. The right means he'll spend the day in discussion under a mango tree with his old friend Charles Reid, a great connoisseur of snail soup. The left is the way to his clinic, in Vialet.

CAMPHOR

Da makes me breathe camphor. I like the smell. It tickles my nose and makes my head spin. I close my eyes to see the yellow lights. Blurry circles with a hard center. I feel as though I'm disappearing into an endless tunnel. I want to touch the source of yellow light. I go further and further in. The yellow light attracts me. I feel weightless. I approach the center of the light. I start to have trouble breathing. But I want to go further. To reach the very heart of yellow. It's incredibly hot. I'm sweating. I feel beads of sweat on my eyelids. I continue my journey toward the seventh circle. It becomes unbearable. I'm going to burn. Yellow fire. Vava's dress. Her big black eyes. HER TERRIBLE BIG BLACK EYES. At the center of the light is a frigid black hole.

EYELIDS

Vava's eyelids. Black butterflies. Two ample wings. Soft, full beating. I'm nauseous. Black. Red. I choose yellow.

THE ROOM

The room smells of camphor. I've worn a cold compress on my head for two days. My fever has subsided. Da doesn't want me to leave the room. She is sitting at my bedside with a coffee pot at her feet. I'm in bed, my head on a mountain of pillows. I feel a little better. Da holds my shoulders up so I can drink a bitter mixture: verbena tea. I can scarcely lift my head. I make a face. Da says that's a good sign.

THE ILLUMINATED VIRGIN

On the little table near the wall that separates the big room from my grandfather's old room is an illuminated picture of the Virgin. Da kneels before the statue every time she crosses the room. The Virgin's arms are spread. Each of her open palms holds a prayer book. Da always begins her litany by reciting the Virgin's different names: Our Lady of Mount Carmel, the Immaculate Conception, Our Lady of Perpetual Help, Mary, Mary, Mother of God. Da closes her eyes to pray. She ends by asking the Virgin to protect her daughters. She speaks their names: "Marie, Raymonde, Renée, Gilberte, Ninine ... Lord, they are in your merciful hands."

Da makes the sign of the cross, then gets heavily to her feet.

TIMISE

Timise, an old cousin of my grandfather's, came in search of gossip. I heard her voice from my room. Her high-pitched voice from the dining room, talking with Da. Timise always makes me think of a bird of prey. More like a vulture. Maybe because of her nose. I saw a picture of a vulture in my geography book. Aunt Timise has a wrinkled little head, a receding chin and no teeth. According to Da, she can break bones with her purple gums. She insists on kissing everyone on the mouth. A mouth filled with cadaverous drool. Whenever I get sick, Timise always shows up, without anyone having to tell her.

HELLFIRE

Timise lives in Petite Guinée, near the swamp, in a house with a thatched roof. She's lived alone there since the death of her only daughter. Besides Da, she hardly knows anyone. Children are afraid of her because of the stained dress she always wears. Sometimes, when the sun is too hot and the streets are deserted, you can see her going up the rue Geffrard. Auguste, Evan, Francis and Dominique hide behind the trees and throw rocks at her. Timise turns on them, threatening them with hellfire. She raises her skeletal arms heavenward and calls upon Saint Matthew. The boys will burn unto the seventh generation.

THREE DROPS

Timise came into my room. She doesn't bother asking me how I am, or where it hurts. She undresses completely, then takes out a big red handkerchief that holds a little vial of castor oil. Timise measures out three drops: one on my forehead, one on my chest, the third on my right foot. Her crooked fingers begin massaging my forehead and my temples. My head begins to burn. She opens my mouth and rubs my gums hard with her dirty finger. She moves down to my neck, and tries to unscrew my head. She takes a penny from her handkerchief and sticks it on my stomach. Timise presses the coin into my solar plexus with all her might. I can't breathe. I can hardly keep from vomiting. Then she turns her attention to my thighs, my ankles and the soles of my feet. Always in search of the bad blood inside me. She repeats the whole business several times, then, finally, her face lights up. She's found it. She leans over me and sucks my skin until it bleeds, at the spot where she had placed the little coin.

THE BATH

At noon, Da put two white tubs full of water under the mango tree, in the sun. Then she went and picked some orange-tree leaves and threw them in the tubs. A heavy, very ripe mango fell near the tub. It didn't take the ants long to find their way into the heart of the fruit. Da came and got me from my room. My legs were still a little weak and my head felt heavy. Da took off my pajamas and helped me climb into the first tub. She washed my hair and lathered my body with cheap-smelling soap. My skin is so fragile I was afraid the soap would tear it. Da rinsed me in the water in the second tub. A few orange leaves were stuck to my head and back. Da didn't brush them off. Marquis started circling the tub, intending to take a bath too. I was so happy to see him I forgot to shoo him away. Then Da wrapped me in a very clean white sheet. We went back to the room and Da opened all the windows to get rid of the smell of fever.

13. LIFE

THE COCK

Borno came past the gallery and nodded a greeting to Da.
I'm sure he's going to a cockfight at Germain's place. The sky
is a hard, clean shade of blue. The warm afternoon air. Borno
is holding the rooster under his arm, its head completely
covered by an old sock. The cock must not know where it's
going. I see its sharp beak sticking through the sock. It keeps
turning its head, this way and that.

"He's a number one rooster, Da. I bought him in the
Dominican Republic ..."

"They do have good roosters there ..."

"What's the matter with him? Is he sick?"

No one ever speaks to me directly.

"He's had a fever for the last three weeks."

"Da, you've got to treat a kid like you would a rooster.
Alcohol's the only remedy. Mix a little starch with some cane
liquor, then smear it all over his body."

"Thank you for the advice, Borno. I'll try it next time."

"I've got some cane liquor with me right now, Da."

"I'll do it tomorrow ... Timise gave him a massage once
already."

"There's nothing like cane liquor, for cocks and boys
alike. Raise that boy like you would a fighting cock. Don't
suffocate him under your skirts, Da."

Borno turns to me and I see his eyes, red from drink and
lack of sleep.

"I bet you've never fought."

I look at him and say nothing.

"Still, he looks like a sly one, Da, this boy of yours."

Da looks at me and smiles. I love her smile. I lean over to watch an ant carrying a tiny piece of bread. I almost touch it with my left eye.

"Do you want a cup of coffee?" Da asks, already filling the blue cup.

Borno takes two steps toward the gallery, picks up the cup and drinks down the coffee in two long, powerful swallows.

"Thanks, Da. Good coffee ... Well, I have to be running now."

Borno pulls the bottle of cane liquor from his right back pocket, takes a long drink, swallows some of it and spits the rest out violently on the rooster's head.

"Believe me," he says, walking away, "if you've got a young boy, you've got to treat him like you would a young cock. Don't coddle him under your skirts, Da."

I watch Borno's back as he goes toward the Croix de la Jubilée. The rooster's head is still wrapped in a sock. Just as Borno was about to turn right in front of Germain's gaming house, Devieux's black car took the corner without sounding its horn. Borno barely sidestepped it.

14. NIGHT

THE WINDOW

When I sleep in my grandfather's room, I always have the same dream. I am in a town I don't recognize. In any case, it's not Petit-Goâve. I don't see the old bald mountain, or Petite Guinée, or the Croix de la Jubilée, or the harbor or the Boys School. I don't see any of those things, yet I feel I'm in Petit-Goâve. I fly over the town. I simply stretch out my arms and take off. I fly over the swamps and into people's houses through their windows.

THE LAMP

A little red house in the distance. Near the Cross. I'm heading for it. The window is open. A lamp on a tiny bedside table. Vava, lying on a little bed with pink sheets. I go into the room. I watch her sleeping for a while. Her breathing is calm. When I bend to kiss her, I see a snake has taken her place. I scream with fright. The snake raises its head sharply. I want to flee the room, but my wings won't work any more.

THE PERFECT NIGHT

Loné the notary walks home with his easy stride. A starry sky. A light breeze. The notary stops.

"A perfect night, Da."

"It is."

And Loné the notary goes on his quiet way.

THE SNAKE

Da told me this story.

This is the story of a girl who was too beautiful to find a husband. She was so beautiful that no man in the town seemed worthy of her. One day, a stranger arrived. He was dressed in black and rode a black horse. His eyes were slightly slanted. The man went immediately to the beautiful girl's house and asked for her hand in marriage. Her mother accepted and the wedding was set for the following Sunday. Everyone in the town was amazed at how quickly the betrothal had occurred. The wedding party was very small; the girl's mother did not have many friends in the town, and the groom had lost his family. The couple spent their wedding night in the little room that had belonged to the bride before her wedding. Her mother was sleeping in the room next door. In the middle of the night, a frightened scream was heard.

"Mama," said the new bride, "there's a snake in my bed."

"That's perfectly normal."

An hour later, she heard, "Mama, mama, the snake is swallowing me ..."

"Now, now, daughter, don't be afraid ..."

A little later came a voice: "Mama, I'm afraid ... I'm going to die ... The snake is swallowing me."

"Now, now, daughter, the same thing happened to me when I was your age ... But you see, I'm very much alive today."

"Mama, it's a real snake ..."

Just to be sure, the mother rose from her bed and went to see what was happening in the nuptial chamber. Her daughter was right: the snake was about to swallow her head. Quickly, the mother grabbed a machete and chopped off the

snake's head. The snake turned into a handsome, head-
less man.

THE ECHO OF HORSESHOES

Da and I sat out on the gallery very late. All the houses on the
street had closed their doors. Even old Nathan's, he who
always stays up late. We heard the pack of dogs that gather at
the foot of the Cross. The street changed color. The pallid
light of midnight. Oginé returned for Chaël Charles' mare in
the park. In the silence of the night, we clearly heard the click
of its horseshoes. When the mare went past the Rigauds' big
wooden house, the sound faded, but I could still see her big
behind swinging like a pendulum.

DA'S DREAM

Da dreamed that Mozart had died. We were to bury him at
four o'clock in the afternoon. Da was sitting on her gallery
when she saw Mozart come hurrying past. He had forgotten
his hat and was returning to the shop to fetch it. Thérèse, his
wife, was filling bags of sugar. Mozart came in, took down
his straw hat and kissed Thérèse on both cheeks. Augereau
tried to stop him to ask some questions about his funeral.
Mozart told him it was still set for four o'clock and that he
was in a hurry to get to Petite Guinée and back by four. Mozart
shook Augereau's hand quickly and ran off to join Passilus,
who was waiting for him by the courthouse. For a moment
Augereau looked at the hand that had shaken Mozart's hand,
then called out to Da that he had things to do at the Croix de
la Jubilée too, but that he hoped to be back for the funeral.
Thérèse came to complain to Da that Mozart had left without
telling her what suit he wanted to wear for the occasion. Da
told her that any black suit would do just fine.

DA'S INTERPRETATION

The hat is the main element in the dream, and hats bring good luck. Mozart is doubly lucky, because dying in a dream is a good sign. It indicates that the person is in good health. Mozart will certainly strike a profitable deal in the next few days. A week after the dream, Mozart won the lottery (the third grand prize) and was able to buy a piece of land in Petite Guinée.

A FISH IN LOVE

Da told me this story.

The story of a fish who lived in a pond near Vialet, on the Miragoâne road. A pond where the water was always dirty, except when Clémentine went there. Tezin, the fish who lived at the bottom of the pond, would swim up to the surface every time he heard Clémentine's voice. *Zin, Zin, my friend Zin,* went the song. And the water would turn clear. Unlike her girlfriends, Clémentine always returned home with a bucket of clean water. One day, a girl noticed what Clémentine was doing. She saw her singing when no one else was listening, a sweet song that ran, *Zin, Zin, my friend Zin.* Then Tezin would swim to the surface and the water miraculously become clear. The jealous girl, who had hidden behind a rock to watch, ran and told Clémentine's father everything. Clémentine has a lover, and he's a fish. Her father listened to the story and said nothing, but already he was thinking of a way to catch them. One day, he asked Clémentine to fetch him some water. She took a bucket and went off to the pond. He knew a shortcut, and he went and hid behind a rock. He watched as Clémentine arrived with the bucket on her head, sat down and began to sing. The water grew clear. The fish poked his head out of the water and Clémentine's father, as fast as lightning, cut off his head with a machete. The pond turned red. Her father brought the fish back home and her mother cooked it, but Clémentine refused to eat. She spent the afternoon sitting on an old wicker chair, crying and singing Tezin's song. The more she sang, the deeper the chair sank into the earth. She sang and cried, sang and cried. The chair continued to sink. Later, her mother heard a faint voice. She looked for her everywhere, and finally found her behind the house. Clémentine had completely sunk into the earth. Only a braid of hair remained above the ground. Her mother yanked on the braid, and it came off in her hand.

COURAGE, ZETTE

Zette started the whole business herself.

"I won't be staying up late tonight, Da."

"Is Charles back?"

"No, Da. I don't know if he's dead or alive."

"Courage, daughter."

"Goodnight, Da."

"Goodnight, Zette."

"See you tomorrow."

"Of course. See you tomorrow."

"This may be my last night, Da."

"Don't lose faith, daughter. Go to bed and the Lord will watch over you."

Zette went inside. A minute later she came out again.

"Da, if I'm not up by eleven, send your boy over to see what's happened."

"Of course, Zette. But I'm sure you'll be fresh as a rose tomorrow morning."

"Thank you, Da. You give me strength."

Every evening, it's the same ritual. Zette is afraid of

dying in her sleep.

GIDEON'S DOG

Once Da saw Gideon, a month after he died. Da knew it was he because that night his dog was following him. The dog didn't live long after Gideon's death. Three months later, he died of heartache. And now Da saw him running behind Gideon.

ZETTE'S DREAM

Zette dreamed that two ladies came visiting. One in blue, the other in white. They arrived at Zette's house and spent the entire afternoon talking together, without ever once inquiring after her, or inviting her to take part in their conversation. Just after the angelus bell, they departed without having spoken a word to her.

DA'S INTERPRETATION

They are the messengers of death. For them, Zette is already dead, even if she's still alive.

BARON SAMEDI

It rained this afternoon, in the middle of a sunny day. Da said Baron Samedi was beating his wife.

"The bastard has nothing else better to do," said Zette.

BROTHER JÉRÔME'S DREAM

Brother Jérôme dreamed of his mother who died nine years ago. He was at home eating a herring when his mother came in through the back door. She was wearing her funeral dress and she looked younger. The way she did in the photograph in the living room, where she is posing with her little sister Iplena.

"How beautiful you look, Mother!" Brother Jérôme marveled as she came in.

"That's how it is, up there, Jérôme. You can choose any age you want to and live in it forever. That was the best time of my life, when I was still on earth: Iplena and I were always together. I hadn't met that bastard father of yours yet ..."

"Why did you come back, Mother?"

"I came back for you, Jérôme. I can't stand to be so happy up there when my only son is living in poverty."

"But everything is fine, Mother. This is my life. When I die, I'll have something else."

"But, Jérôme, it's a waste of time ... You can't imagine the happiness awaiting you up there."

"I'll discover it in due time, Mother."

"Jérôme, I've come for you and I won't leave without you."

"Can you wait until I've finished this herring, Mother?"

His mother sat down, while Brother Jérôme calmly went on eating his herring.

DA'S INTERPRETATION

That woman wasn't his mother. She was the goddess Erzulie who had dressed herself in Jérôme's mother's features. She wants to be Jérôme's mistress, and when the goddess Erzulie makes up her mind about a man, nothing can stop her. One day, Jérôme will be hers. No man can resist Erzulie.

AUGEREAU'S DREAM

Augereau dreamed a dog bit him.

DA'S INTERPRETATION

There's a good chance that Augereau will be bitten by Marquis this week.

SLEEP

Da goes into the house with her chair. I put the little bench against the wall. Then Da locks the front door. She goes through the living room and turns off the light. I get undressed and climb right into bed. I always sleep curled up with a pillow against my chest. Da gets undressed too. I clearly see her back, all stained with big strawberry marks. Da lies down, but I know she is waiting for me to fall asleep before she drifts off. Da always falls asleep after I do and wakes up first. I have never seen her sleeping. I feel sleep start out from the tips of my toes and climb up my spine, then nestle warmly against the nape of my neck.

PART III

15. GIRLS

DIDI

I was with Frantz when I met Didi near the soccer field. The big field where I go to watch Camelo on Sundays. Frantz said hi to Didi. I didn't because she's my cousin. She lives near the market. I already saw her once this afternoon, at recess. She goes to the Sisters of Wisdom. Right across from my school. We see each other every day, during recess or after school. Sometimes Da gives me an orange or mango for Didi. When she does, I go to the gate, the one that opens onto the rue La-Justice, and Didi comes out to meet me. She's always with a girlfriend. Vava, sometimes. Sylphise or Zina, other times.

LOVE

Didi is in love with Frantz. I know, because she never looks at him. She acts as though he doesn't exist.

Vava does the same thing with me, but it's not for the same reason.

WAITING

Didi wants me to stay. She's waiting for her friends. Frantz and I are supposed to go to La Hatte to get a geography book that Frantz lent to Rico. I'm not too fond of the idea. I know Vava is going to come along. I clown around to pass the time. Frantz pulls on my sleeve. Vava is taking her time.

DUST

I was trying to get a speck of dust out of Frantz's left eye when I heard Vava's voice right behind me.

"What's the matter with him?"

Zina jumped on Frantz immediately and practically tore out his eye. Frantz retreated from the Fury.

"Let me try," Vava said.

She made Frantz stand sideways to her and breathed into his eye, so close I thought she had kissed him. Frantz rubbed his eyes. The speck of dust was gone.

Sylphise wanted to know where we were going.

"If you're going to Petite Guinée," she said, "that's my way too."

"No, we're going in the other direction."

Sylphise gave me a black look. She's in love with Frantz too.

REMORSE

Marquis showed up, tail wagging, rubbing against my legs. I gave him a good kick in the ribs. He scurried off, yelping. I felt a twinge of remorse. I don't understand why I have a dog that's so ugly. No one ever picks him up. Except me.

16. THE GRANDMOTHER

Frantz and I climbed the steep slope to La Hatte. There are plenty of luxurious houses on both sides of the street. Rico lives further up, almost to the foot of Tapion Mountain. His house stands all by itself, just past the big white one that belongs to the American pastor. Rico's house is hidden by a tuft of short mango trees. The spring flows a few meters from it. People come from far away, as far as Miragoâne, for its water. Rich people like the Devieux, the Bombaces, the Reyers and Pastor Jones. Loné the notary from the rue Desvignes will drink only water from the spring. Rico's mother sells it in big hollow gourds.

THE GRANDMOTHER

Rico lives with his brother Ricardi, his mother and his blind grandmother. His grandmother feels all, hears all, knows all. Rico motioned to us not to make any noise, to really walk on our tiptoes.

"Who goes there?" his grandmother challenged us.

Rico put his finger on his lips.

"Oh, it's you, Frantz. Come in."

Frantz went in. I stayed in the doorway.

"Why are you standing there? Come in, we're not going to eat you. How's your grandmother?"

"Fine, thank you," I said, amazed she had recognized

me before I opened my mouth. And I don't even come here very often.

Rico smiled. He knew his grandmother would recognize us. Rico always says that she sees better than people who have eyes. I told Da that, and Da said it was because she was born blind.

"Come here ... Come closer," she said in a voice a little more cordial than before.

Still, I kept my distance.

"You know I was at school with your grandmother. We were good friends back then. She was really crazy about Odilon. Whatever became of him, anyway?"

"He's selling hay to Oginé now."

She was silent a moment or two.

"Odilon," she said. "Odile Lauredan, selling hay ... Who would have believed it ..."

I examined her dirty nails and her big eyes that see only darkness.

"Don't look at me like that," she said in a loud voice that froze me. "If it weren't for me, you wouldn't be here ..."

"What do you mean?" Rico asked for me.

She took her time, as if assembling her thoughts.

"I delivered your grandmother ... The husband wasn't even there. Timise and I helped that poor unfortunate woman give birth. It was her first child. Your mother, I believe. What did that tyrant ever become, anyway? He did so much harm to that poor woman. I hope he's dead. Is he?"

"Yes."

"May he rest in peace ... And good riddance."

"Grandmother," said Rico, "you're talking about his grandfather."

"I know it, and I don't owe the bastard a thing. I never gave in to him and I'm the only one of us who didn't. I hope Da knows that ... Besides, the old letch never hid a thing ... He had sneaky hands, always with a pat on your backside ... But all that belongs to the past ... Even if he did do that woman a lot of harm ... Now, everyone is dead. I know men: one minute they're eight years old, the next minute they're dead ... I loved Odilon too ... Did anyone ever tell you his story?"

"Yes."

"Who?"

"Da."

"She must have told it her way ... I'm going to tell you the real story of Odilon Lauredan, king of hearts ..."

Rico's grandmother was still talking when we left the house. Still sitting in the same spot, in the dark corner. Her face was invisible. Only her big eyes shone.

17. THE CHICKEN THIEF

CHICKENS

We climbed the wall and jumped into Francillon's yard. Behind the old lyceum that had fallen into ruin. Frantz listened carefully. Everything was quiet. Francillon was sitting in front, on his gallery, with his wife. Frantz told me to go and distract him while he tried to catch a chicken.

"How come you're limping like that?" Francillon asked me.

"A nail. I stepped on a nail."

"Come, I'll disinfect it."

"Thank you, but you don't have to ... I'll go home instead ..."

Francillon came down from his gallery. He moved toward me. The gate was closed. Timidly, I retreated.

"Come here. I told you I would fix it."

I turned to run. Francillon caught me by the arm. His hands were like vises.

"Hold him, Solange, I'll take care of the other one in the yard ... You little rascals, you'll never fool me twice."

He shouted so loud that Frantz heard him and had the time to escape. I got away from his wife by kicking her hard in the shins. Frantz and I caught up with each other on the rue Dessalines, by the bakery.

THE GEOGRAPHY LESSON

Tomorrow's geography lesson is on the mountainous regions

in the Département de l'Ouest. Over and over, Da makes me recite the names: Hospital Mountain, Lost Children Mountain, the Black Mountains.

"Why do they call it Lost Children Mountain, Da? Did some children get lost there?"

"I don't know ... Ask your teacher."

"He'll just say I was sleeping when he covered the lesson."

"Maybe you were sleeping."

"No, Da. He's the one who does the sleeping. He comes into class and tells us to start reciting the lesson. We all get up and take turns reciting, and the next thing we know, he's snoring."

Da frowns.

"What do you do when that happens?"

"We have to be extra careful when we recite, because if we ever miss a word in the lesson, he wakes up and starts screaming, like he was having a nightmare."

THE HISTORY LESSON

My history lesson is on the Battle of Vertières. The final battle the black army fought with the French. General Capoix-la-mort was leading the Twenty-Fourth Half-Brigade when a cannonball knocked off his hat. "Advance, advance!" cried Capoix. A second cannonball blew his horse from underneath him. "Advance, advance!" he cried again. Faced with such bravery, the French General Rochambeau asked for a cease-fire. He sent a detachment of officers to present honors to the black officer who had distinguished himself so magnificently.

THE BROOM

I found an old hat in my grandfather's room. With a new broom for a horse, I recited my lesson for Da.

"Advance, advance!" I shouted at the top of my lungs. Da loves that lesson. She often asks me to repeat it. I put on my hat and saddle up my handsome broom again.

"Advance, advance ..."

Da smiles.

THE ACCUSATION

I was beginning my history lesson for the tenth time when I spotted Francillon coming up the street, his straw hat in his hand. Capoix-la-mort had picked himself up from the enemy cannonballs for the second time when Francillon climbed the steps onto our gallery.

"Da, I am here to tell you to keep an eye on your boy."

"What's the matter, Francillon?"

"Da, he and another boy tried to steal a chicken from me."

"He did? Are you sure you saw him, Francillon?"

"I saw what I saw, Da."

"Look at him, Francillon. He's been studying his lessons here all afternoon."

Francillon looked at me for the first time. He scrutinized me with his rheumy eyes. I considered the sky. A pretty pink kite was floating above the town reservoir. After a while, Francillon looked back at Da.

"You don't seem very sure, Francillon ..."

He ran his hand through his hair.

"The problem is, Da, they all look the same ..."

"You mean you came and interrupted my son's lessons to tell me he looks like a chicken thief?"

Francillon had no choice but to retreat.

"Da, I know it's only a chicken, and all kids do that for fun ... I never take them to court, or to the barracks ..."

"Francillon, how do you expect me to punish him if

you don't remember what happened ... Maybe you have him mixed up with another boy ..."

"I have to go now, Da. I absolutely need to talk to Passilus this evening, and I believe I just saw him getting on his bicycle to go."

"Won't you have a cup of coffee?"

"Another time, Da."

Once Francillon was gone, Da turned to me.

"You go inside. You have some explaining to do about what you were up to in Francillon's henhouse."

18. THE GAME

THE EAGLE

Camelo walked across Naréus' gallery with nothing but a towel around his waist. He's going swimming in the big pool behind Gisèle's house. I know because I'm supposed to soap up his back. Camelo is my favorite player. My idol. He plays in goal for my team, the Black Eagles. He's the eagle himself. He can catch any shot in mid-air. Sometimes I think he really does have wings. I'm meeting Frantz and Rico at three o'clock this afternoon on the field.

SOAP

Gisèle came up behind me and took the soap out of my hands.

"You can go now … I'll take care of him," she said.

I pretended I was leaving. First I went around the house, then I climbed on top of Naréus' trellis. You can see everything from there.

THE BEAUTIFUL NURSE

Gisèle isn't married. But she has a child. An ugly girl who goes to the National Girls School, near the rue Dessalines. Fifi is as skinny as a wire and has a mouthful of braces. According to Naréus, Gisèle is a free woman. Like all nurses, added Willy Bony, Augereau's friend. I can rub Camelo's back better than she can. Gisèle is too gentle when she runs the soap over him. Camelo closes his eyes even when there's no soap on his face. I can tell he doesn't like the way Gisèle does it. Gisèle sings as she lathers his hair. I know Camelo doesn't like that. He makes faces when Gisèle's red nails sink into his scalp. Camelo draws her closer in the pool. She screams without making a sound. She opens her mouth wide like a fish. Her green dress floats on the water. She presses herself against Camelo. They stay that way for a long time until Camelo starts trembling too.

THE TICKET

Frantz and Rico were waiting for me at the entrance to the soccer field. Frantz thought for sure we could get in without paying. All three of us would go in together to try to confuse the ticket-taker by talking at the same time. Father Magloire has been guarding the gate for thirty-odd years, and has had time to get a little hard of hearing.

"Father Magloire, what teams are playing today?" asked Frantz.

"What? What did you say?"

We didn't give Father Magloire time to answer.

"Has the game started yet, Father Magloire?"

He turned to Rico and cocked his hand around his ear.

"The game, Father Magloire."

"What game?" he shouted.

"Today's game."

"What is it you want to know?" Father Magloire shouted his question.

Before Rico could ask the question, I interrupted.

"Did Camelo show up yet, Father Magloire?"

Three people were waiting behind us to buy their tickets. They were starting to get impatient. Father Magloire insisted on answering our questions. The people wanted to pay their admission and go in, especially since the game had started ten minutes ago. Frantz and Rico took advantage of the confusion to slip discreetly past Father Magloire.

THE LOST TICKET

I waited by the gate. From time to time, Father Magloire would gaze at me with his piercing eyes. As if he were remembering something. Not only is Father Magloire hard of hearing, his memory has some holes in it, too. In the old days, Camelo said, he was the best soccer player Petit-Goâve ever knew. He scored the winning goal in the historic game against Miragoâne, forty years ago. Father Magloire looked at me without recognizing me. Fortunately, Frantz came up. He asked Father Magloire for an exit pass. He told him he'd be coming right back. Frantz went out and handed me the pass. I put on a hat and went in. Father Magloire didn't notice a thing. Two minutes later, Frantz showed up at the gate, and Father Magloire asked him for his pass.

"I just went out, Father Magloire ... I lost my pass, right around here, somewhere ..."

"If you don't have a ticket, there's nothing I can do for you, son."

"Look at me, Father Magloire, don't you remember, I just asked you for a pass."

Frantz pretended to search his pockets again.

"All right, you can go in."

THE YELLOW JERSEY

We ran toward the crowd. Everyone was standing at the edge of the field. The Black Eagles were wearing the yellow jersey. We had almost reached the field when an explosion of voices knocked us to the ground. The Tigers, our adversaries from La Hatte, just scored a goal. Rico leapt for joy, but Frantz and I felt sick. Semephen, the Tigers' dangerous forward, scored it. They call him the Tiger. The Tiger beat the Eagle. I pushed my way through the forest of legs. I saw Camelo's bloody face. People were yelling. Semephen was going down left wing again, dribbling past Occlève, cutting back toward mid-field and Killick, the Black Eagles' great defensive back. Big Killick, as solid as a rock. Semephen against Killick. I could hear the breathing of the crowd. Semephen faked right, then threw Killick off stride by cutting to the left. Semephen streaked in alone toward Camelo's goal. The crowd's heart stopped beating. Semephen raised his left foot to shoot from ten meters out. With a desperate leap, the Eagle darted toward the Tiger's feet and stripped the ball from him. A yellow card went twirling into the air. The match ended in a one-to-nothing Tiger victory, but Camelo's stop is what people remembered. Even Saint-Vil Mayard, the barber of the rue Lamarre, talked about it.

"In thirty years, I've never seen anything like it, Loné. He flew through the air, in broad daylight, like an eagle … He truly is Duvivier's son, a devil through and through."

"In my opinion," Loné the notary answered, "Camelo is a very quick goalie who practiced for this most important match. The Eagles lost, but Camelo is the hero of the day."

THE HERO

Camelo swept by me without seeing me. On his arm was pretty Gisèle, who glanced at me from over her shoulder. I know the reason the team lost today: it's because of what happened in the pool this afternoon. I'm the only one who knows.

THE BUTTON

Frantz punched a guy from the National Boys School who was displaying his happiness a little too openly. Since he was with a friend, I had to fight too. We ended up in the grass. When we got up a minute later, we realized that Frantz had lost a button from his shirt. We searched for ten minutes. In the end, the guy found the button that had gotten stuck in my hair.

THE LITTLE WALL

Da gave me money to buy my ticket to the game. I still have that money. I never pay for a Black Eagles match. I just sit on the little wall by the gate and wait for Camelo. When he comes, I run over and take his soccer shoes, which he never wears before a game. I tie the laces together and throw the shoes around my neck. Then I go in behind him, as if I were a player too, or his replacement. When we go past Father Magloire, Camelo always puts his arm around my shoulder. That way, we go in together. Today, Camelo showed up with Gisèle, and his arm was around her neck.

STONES

After the game, Frantz and I walked down to the market. Rico left us near the hospital. He doesn't like to go home in the dark. Frantz and I strolled through the night market. The vendors had started lighting their lamps. Frantz brought me down to the sea, not far from where the fish-ladies have their counters. The smell always makes me nauseous. Frantz threw a few stones in the water, and they skipped like flying fish. I went and vomited on the beach.

PART IV

19. THE SEA

THE FIRST TIME

I remember the first time I saw the sea. A dozen days after my birth. It must have been the first day I went onto the gallery in my mother's arms. My mother loved the sea. From our gallery, we can see it.

BLUE

Da always says that the sky is blue because of the sea. For a long time I thought the sea and the sky were one. The sea has fishes. The sky, stars. Rain is the proof that the sky is liquid.

INK

Da told me the story of Adrien, a man from the Second Plain. He arrived in town at noon. He saw the sea for the first time. Adrien walked through the market to see it from close up. He walked into the water fully dressed and emerged soaking wet. He was disappointed. Adrien had thought it was made out of ink.

THE HARBOR

My grandfather took me to the harbor for the first time. That's where I saw the sea from close up. Willy Bony was working at Customs. He asked my grandfather if this was really the first time I had come here. When my grandfather

answered yes, he took off my shoes and led me onto the jetty.
My grandfather asked Willy Bony to bring me to Bombace's
afterward. That's where he would be for the day.

MY BIG TOE

I first knew the sea through my left big toe. I was sitting
on the far end of the jetty. Despite all my efforts, I couldn't
touch the water. Willy Bony took me by the arm and let me
slip gently into the sea.

20. NOON

A little launch crossed in front of us with a dozen people on board. Some wore their handkerchiefs on their heads to protect against the sun. They were going to La Gonave for salt and mahogany.

"You've got to be back by five o'clock!" Willy Bony shouted to them.

"We'll be there, Director."

"We're expecting a ship today, you know ..."

"Of course, Director. The *Hollandais*."

"Godspeed!"

"Thank you, Director."

And they began to sing:

> *Sou lanmè mouin rélé Agoué*
> *Nan Zilé mal rélé Agoué ...*

THE DROWNED MAN

Da is afraid of the water. One of her brothers drowned as she watched, helpless. He was on the boat returning from Jérémie. He died in the harbor. Da had come to meet him. The boat was coming in. Everyone in the town watched it sink like a stone. Firmin, Da's younger brother, didn't know how to swim. Da yelled to the people going to save the victims that Firmin couldn't swim. Fedor, Semephen's father, said they had to save the women and children first.

The boat came back without Firmin. Fedor told us his last words: "Tell Da to take the cover off the pot if she doesn't want the soup to spoil."

NOON

The sun was at its zenith. You couldn't see your shadow under the water. Willy Bony was walking with me through the harbor. I saw my shadow underfoot.

"What do fish do at noon?"

"It's lunchtime."

"For fish too?"

"For everybody."

"What do they eat?"

"Fish," Willy Bony told me.

"But it's not even Friday."

Willy Bony burst out laughing.

THE OFFICE

Willy Bony had me sit at the desk that was his when he was assistant-director. It's Lejeune's desk now. He was on the boat going to La Gonave. Willy Bony asked me to wait for him. He told me he had a few minutes of work. In the meantime, I inspected the premises. A large blotter by an inkwell with violet ink. Other inkwells, closed tight, sit on the desk. In the left corner is an open notebook with fine blue and red lines. Lejeune has good handwriting. He's especially good with numbers. Each page is divided in two. The category "Arrivals" and the category "Departures." Two columns of figures under each category. Every page is signed by Willy Bony, Customs Director, Petit-Goâve, and André Lejeune, Assistant-Director.

THE MEAL

Willy Bony came into the room, followed by an old woman, older than Da, even older than Cornélia. The most wrinkled face I've ever seen. She was carrying a tray of food. Willy Bony took the plates from her hands before it was too late. He set a well-filled plate before me. A nice threadfin with a long banana and a little white rice moistened with onion sauce on the side. I ate everything as I watched the sea.

SIESTA

Right after his coffee, Willy Bony fell like a ton of bricks. His head on his desk.

"I think I'll get some shut-eye," he said.

I don't know how long we slept. The noise of the men returning from La Gonave woke us up.

THE BOAT

The men were ready when the *Hollandais* pulled into the bay. Willy Bony asked me to go on board ship with him. In the launch that took us to it, I sat next to Grégoire, Zina's father. He told me to put my hand in the water. With my palm open. The whole time I was sure the fish were going to eat my hand, because they knew I had just eaten one of their friends.

When I got back, my grandfather was waiting for me in Willy Bony's office.

21. THE THEOREMS

THEOREM I

Saint-Vil Mayard, the barber of the rue Lamarre, was in the middle of cutting Willy Bony's hair when he stated the first of his theorems: "A body immersed in water tends to emerge wet."

Loné the notary, who was waiting his turn, rose to salute the achievement.

"There, Saint-Vil, my friend, you've got us good. No one can deny that."

THEOREM II

One week later.

This time, Loné the notary was alone in Saint-Vil Mayard's barbershop. Passilus was pretending to read a newspaper on the gallery as he waited his turn. Despite everything he was to say later, Passilus heard nothing.

Saint-Vil Mayard, visibly stimulated by his initial success, declared in a peremptory tone: "A body immersed in water, if it does not surface after two hours, must be assumed to be lost."

"Why two hours?"

"Because ..."

"Why not a more reasonable period of time?"

"... it's two hours."

"It seems to me ..."

"A theorem cannot be discussed, Loné."

THEOREM III

The following day, all the same.

Saint-Vil Mayard wanted to quickly correct the second theorem in order to avoid a plethora of erroneous interpretations.

This time, he stated definitively: "A body immersed in water in the vicinity of a shark, if it does not surface after two hours, must be assumed to be lost."

Finally, unanimity was established around the issue. Augereau, Willy Bony's friend, took the floor.

"My friends," said Augereau, "it may well be that Saint-Vil Mayard is the Archimedes of Petit-Goâve, but I doubt whether Archimedes would ever be considered the Saint-Vil Mayard of Athens."

After a moment of silence granted the audience to digest this thought, Loné the notary added the summing-up.

"True enough, Augereau. But you must admit that the comparison is, nevertheless, flattering."

In unison, the group applauded Saint-Vil Mayard for the originality and audacity of his thought processes.

22. FRIENDS

THE POSTMAN

Every Tuesday, the Port-au-Prince paper is delivered to Passilus. Lupcius, Occlève's brother, brings it to him. Which is normal, since he's the postman. Da says that Lupcius should not have the job. He bears too many grudges. When he gets angry at someone, to punish him, he won't deliver his mail for an entire month. Once, Zette received no mail for three months because of her dog. Zette has a little dog that never barks at anyone. It's always lying on her gallery. Lupcius claims he's afraid of her dog. And even after Zette got rid of it, Lupcius still preferred to hand over Zette's mail to Mozart. He said the dog could come back at any time, since a dog never forgets its home. And that's true, because Marquis found my bed after months of being away.

THE NEWSPAPER

I read the newspaper for Passilus on Tuesday afternoons. Which is convenient, since we never have homework for Wednesday. On Wednesdays, half the day is spent pulling out weeds in the schoolyard. So, on Tuesdays, I can read the newspaper for Passilus. He doesn't know how to read. When his friends come to visit in the evenings, he acts as if he had read the paper himself. Passilus gives me 20 centimes for the news, 25 centimes for the long articles on page four (about electricity, the water shortage in the Northwest *département*, malnutrition in the Port-au-Prince slums, the Catholic church's campaign against voodoo, etc.), and 5 centimes extra if I read the advertisements.

FRIENDS

Even Loné the notary stops by to see Passilus from time to time. There are always half a dozen chairs on the gallery. My grandfather used to go there too. They're talking politics, Da tells me. Every time some trouble happens in Port-au-Prince, the police come and arrest Passilus and his friends. The raids always happen at night. The next morning, there is not a man left in the town.

A PINK SKY

Passilus lives just this side of the Croix de la Jubilée. From here, I can see everything that happens on his gallery perfectly well. Sometimes Da asks me if I can see my grandfather.

"Yes, Da."

"Who's he with?"

"He's sitting with the government commissioner, Willy Bony, Lupcius the postman, Cephas, Augereau and Saint-Vil Mayard."

"What are they doing?"

"Passilus is talking and a lady is serving coffee to everyone."

"What's your grandfather doing?"

"He's scratching the back of his head."

"All right, go inside now."

Loné the notary always stands in the street, as if he were about to leave at any minute. But he's always the last to go.

Afternoon ends, evening begins. The color of the sky is pink. The air smells like manure.

THE JOURNEY

One day at noon, Saint-Vil Mayard gathered the townspeople together in the harbor to demonstrate his theorem. According to Saint-Vil Mayard, Labarre the fat man should float, despite his three hundred pounds. A small launch took the jury composed of Augereau, Passilus, Loné the notary and Gisèle the nurse (Camelo's mistress), not to mention Jérôme and Willy Bony. The group set out for l'Ilet, across from the harbor. An hour later, the boat came back to pick up Fedor, Cephas, Labarre the fat man and Saint-Vil Mayard himself. Several other persons took seats in the craft to fill it up and keep the weight from being too heavy on one side. Légype (the champion swimmer) swam his way across.

THE RETURN

Night had already fallen when the launch reached the harbor. Total darkness. Everyone looked soaked to the skin.

Complete and utter failure.

"Theories should never be put into practice," is all Loné the notary would say.

23. THE DOGFISH

A WHITE DOG

Légype had his left forearm bitten off by a dogfish. A sea animal with the body of a dog (four legs and a tail) and the head of a shark. Love Léger saw the animal once when he was fishing across from the old fort that dates back to the Indian days. Love Léger is the only person in Petit-Goâve to possess a diving suit. The captain of the *Hollandais* gave it to him as a gift, back when he was director of Customs, before Willy Bony. Léger likes to go fishing in those dangerous waters. He was near the deep water when he heard a barking sound. He wheeled around and saw a dog coming toward him. A white dog. For a moment he thought it was on land, that it was Gideon's dog. As it came closer, moving its legs as if they were fins, he could see its shark mouth. A mouth that was wide open. Love Léger surfaced quickly and managed to get out of the water by swimming up through the steep rocks of the old fort.

THE LEFT ARM

Légype wasn't as lucky as Love Léger. By the time he heard the barking sound, the dogfish was on top of him. He used his left hand to try and surface, but the dog had already fastened onto it. He felt nothing, and managed to surface immediately, escaping with his arm and a half. Doctor Cayemitte had to perform an operation at once to avoid gangrene. Ever since, Légype has been searching for the dogfish to kill it. Wherever he goes, he carries a little knife.

ZETTE'S VERSION

Zette told Da the dog came from Holland, and that it had followed a ship all the way to Port-au-Prince. From Port-au-Prince, it changed ships and followed *La Sirène,* Dinasse's old boat, to Petit-Goâve.

"Why Petit-Goâve, Zette?" asked Loné the notary, with his usual irony.

"How should I know? What matters is that no one can deny that it has entered the gates of our town. And it's here to stay, it seems ..."

"But we still don't know why it chose Petit-Goâve," Loné the notary countered.

"Because, in Holland, the dogfish all know that Loné the notary lives in Petit-Goâve."

"Typically Haitian! No analysis, no debate is possible. Haitians take everything personally."

"Why wouldn't I take it personally? You're talking to me, as far as I can tell, Loné."

The notary gave a big throaty laugh.

"Not at all. I was talking to the dogfish."

"I wouldn't be surprised, coming from a man who can walk in the rain without getting wet."

"Ah, yes, the celebrated relation between science and magic ..."

"Notary Loné, you can use all the big words you want if that's what pleases you, but everyone knows you're a devil, with a particular taste for young children. You're the one who ate Thérèse's baby ..."

This time, Zette went a little too far. Loné the notary

put his hat on his head and went to leave. But, as always, he insisted on having the last word.

"Sometimes, Da, I wonder what came over me to be born in this backward town, when I could just as well have been born in Paris, or Vienna, in Athens or Düsseldorf, or even, if all those cities were taken, in Lisbon. Poor Lisbon ..."

"What do you mean, 'poor Lisbon'?"

"Yes, Da, poor Lisbon."

WILLY BONY'S VERSION

This animal doesn't come from a foreign country. You can believe me, I'm the Customs director. Just because we don't have a giant steel-and-glass building, people think we're not doing our job. My considered opinion, Da, is that the dogfish is from right here. Yes, Da, from Petit-Goâve itself. It hasn't always been a dogfish. Perhaps it's someone among us, who used to walk down the street like you and I, Da, who talked, yes, who talked, who ate meat and went to Mass on Sunday. Despite what everyone says, I don't believe it's Saint-Vil Mayard.

LOVE LÉGER'S VERSION

It's Gideon's dog. Just take a look at the people it's attacked so far. Messidor, Montilas' brother, Légype, Galbaud, that man from Petite Guinée, Camelo, who wasn't injured, Borno and me. We've all had run-ins with Gideon. Légype, it turns out, beat him up in the harbor because of some business about castor oil that no one has ever quite understood. I don't know about Messidor, but Montilas had threatened to melt him down in his old smithy because he hung around his daughter too much. Borno slapped him one Saturday night at Germain's gaming house. Borno's rooster was about to leap at Gideon's Dominican cock when Gideon pulled it out of the ring. Borno saw red. He grabbed the cock out of Gideon's hands and wrung its neck. Gideon got mad, and Borno slapped him. Gideon left, swearing revenge, and that if he couldn't do it, someone else would. As for Camelo, it must have something to do with soccer. Gideon was playing for the Jubilée Lions when Camelo made a fool of him on the field, in front of the civil, military and religious authorities of the town. He let Gideon break in on goal, only to leap for the ball and take it off his feet at the last minute. Even Camelo's fans thought he'd gone a little too far. You don't do that, even to your worst enemy. Nobody knows why the dogfish attacked Galbaud. But if you listen hard enough, you're sure to hear the answer.

24. THE AUTOMOBILE

TWO CARS

Oginé was going past our gallery and called out to Da that Galbaud's car had just arrived from Port-au-Prince. The car was being driven by the dealer's mechanic, since Galbaud didn't know how to drive. Counting Devieux's black car, that will make two of the machines in Petit-Goâve.

"Da, we can't have two cars in this town."

"Tell me why, Oginé."

"For instance, Da, when one car is going up the rue Lamarre and the other is in town and wants to go down the same street, what will happen? They'll run into each other, Da."

"Not necessarily, Oginé. Look, you have five horses with you without having that sort of accident."

"But, Da, a car is not an animal. The horse knows its way."

"Yes, Oginé, but the car is driven by a man who also knows his way."

"Not Galbaud, Da."

THE SHOW

According to Zette, Galbaud's car is running the show, not Galbaud.

"His wife always ran the show too, Da."

"An automobile is not a woman, Zette."

"Yes, Da, but a man is always a man."

"Now, that's true."

THE SECRET DRIVER

Galbaud was seen veering off the road into a sugar-cane field.

"That's normal," remarked Passilus, "since Gideon is driving the car."

"Gideon is dead."

"What difference does that make, Da?"

Old Cornélia, who sees what others cannot see, said there is always another person sitting next to Galbaud, but she can't make out who it is. One thing's for sure: Galbaud is not alone in that car of his. Why else would the car refuse to go near the cemetery?

DEEP WATER

Légype found Galbaud at the bottom of the sea. He was still behind the wheel of his car. His eyes wide open. The dogfish was circling around the Ford.

PART V

25. THE BICYCLE

THE GATES

Rico was waiting for Sylphise at the schoolyard door, by the gate across from Doc's garage.

Sister Noel came onto the balcony and pulled like crazy on the bell-chord. A moment of silence followed. Then, suddenly, an explosion was heard.

Sister Noel's voice.

"Quiet, or no one leaves."

Another moment of silence. Then the noise swelled up again. The gates had opened for good.

THE OLD JUNKER

Frantz pulled up on a bicycle. His brother Ludner's bike. An old black junker that's always breaking down because its chain is too loose. Frantz is forever repairing it. It's the old bike his father gave to Ludner when he bought himself a new Robin Hood from Fabrien. To slow down, he has to put his right foot on the front wheel. Besides, the handlebars are all crooked. Frantz looks as if he's always turning left. He and his brother are the only ones who know how to drive that junk heap.

THE MOST HANDSOME

Finally the girls show up. Zina, my cousin Didi, Vava and Sylphise. Rico loves Sylphise. I love Vava. I have the feeling

that Zina, my cousin Didi, Sylphise and even Vava are all
crazy about Frantz. I can hardly be jealous of Frantz because,
if I were them, I'd feel the same way. Frantz is the most
handsome, the most charming, the cleverest of us all. He has
eyes that kill.

HANDLEBARS

Frantz invented a kind of hook that he installed on the
handlebars of his bicycle. That way, he can keep a book
open in front of him. He can study anywhere. Often, we
meet near the National Boys School or, sometimes, behind
the church. Frantz rides up with his book hooked onto the
handlebars of his old junker. Now and then, he glances over
the chapter that he's studying. Sometimes, we all gather
around him to try to solve an arithmetic problem. We usually
do that in the morning, right in the schoolyard.

FATHER

His father—his mother is dead—doesn't take care of him.
Georges Coutard, Frantz's father, is always hanging out at
Germain's place with a fighting cock under his arm. He's
Borno's friend. The two of them have been together since
childhood. If you talk to Borno, Da says, you might as well
have talked to Georges. According to Zette, who's always
been in love with him, Georges Coutard is a charming man
who simply wasn't made for life's responsibilities.

HYGIENE

The only thing on which Georges Coutard will make no
compromises is cleanliness. If he ran into Frantz in the street
with his hair uncombed, he would kill him. When he meets

him somewhere, he inspects his nails, nose, teeth, ears and armpits. If he is happy with the results of the inspection, he might give him all the money he has in his pockets. But, on the other hand, if Frantz's teeth aren't clean, or his ears or nails haven't been looked after, he drags him by the scruff of his neck through the town, shouting that he's going to throw him into the sea. Which he does.

THE FRAME

Zina climbed onto the frame of the bicycle, in front of Frantz, who was steering. She couldn't stop laughing. The bicycle goes zigzagging down the street, then finally straightens its course. Frantz speeds up, travels two blocks, then returns to the group. Frantz drops Zina off and now it's my cousin Didi's turn. All the girls are waiting to go for a ride. Soon it will be Vava's turn. My heart is in my throat. Why am I not Frantz?

PAIN

I see the nape of her neck riding against Frantz's head. My stomach hurts. The pain is unbearable. My palms are wet. If Vava does not get off that bicycle right now, I think I'm going to lose consciousness. A light breeze rustles the leaves. A kite flies, carefree, in the pure blue sky. My knees tremble. I have become deaf. I have lost my reasoning. All I see is Vava's yellow dress that all but brushes the ground. Vava jumps off the bicycle; she has just seen her mother on Clara's gallery. Fortunately, her mother wasn't looking in our direction. Vava runs through Abraham's yard, toward her house. Just as she went through her door, she turned and waved to us. Frantz pretended to ride in pursuit of her. Clara's dog came running up, yelping. Frantz tried to get away. His feet got caught in the chain. Vava burst out laughing. Everyone is laughing. Even Frantz, who lost his balance because of Clara's little dog.

26. ZOUNE'S COFFEE

A DEAD RAT

I went through the yard and into the house. Frantz and Rico continued on their way. I am going to meet them later in the evening, at the market or by Doc's garage. Marquis came running toward me with something in his mouth, which he laid at my feet. A dead rat. I touched it with the toe of my shoe. Its belly was soft and furry. I put all my weight on its belly. Its mouth opened and let out a little cry.

MANGOS

Da gave me half a dozen juicy mangos and I ate them in the yard, near Chaël Charles' old shack. I took off my shirt first to keep from staining it. Afterward, I washed my mouth and hands and went to see Da on the gallery.

THE METAL BOX

Da sent me to buy coffee at Zoune's.

"Tell Zoune not to mix the coffee with chicory."

I ran like the wind. With Marquis behind me. He looks terrible when he runs that way, throwing his rear end off to the side, as if he were moving two ways at once. Marquis is not going to win the race. Zoune lives on the rue Desvignes, behind Pastor Doll's house. I knocked at her window. She took her time opening it. She wiped the corner of her mouth with the back of her hand. Zoune always smells of herring.

With a deathbed voice, she asked, "What do you want?"

"Coffee."

"Who sent you?"

"Da."

Her eyes lit up.

"She said not to mix the coffee with chicory."

Zoune nodded her head. She got out a big metal box, an old caramel candy box, took a little spoon and put five spoonfuls of coffee in a little brown bag. She gave it to me, then closed the window again.

Marquis pulled up just then, his belly dragging, his tongue hanging out. A distant second.

THE TASTE OF COFFEE

Da took the bag from me, opened it and spent a long time breathing in the coffee. She looked at me and smiled, then took a pinch of it and put it on her tongue.

Da closed her eyes.

27. SHAME

ANGER

A woman in black was coming up the rue Lamarre, with an iron grip on her son's arm. Auguste's mother.

"Wait till we get to the house ... You'll see ..."

"But, Mother, he's lying ... I never miss school."

"Ah, he's lying now ... We'll see about that ... I make sacrifices to send you to school and now they tell me you haven't been there for the last month ... I bought you books, a uniform, not to mention the money I had to spend for this expense and that, your share of the globe they were buying, the big classroom ruler you broke and I had to replace ... And now I learn, just by chance, that you haven't been to school for a month ... We'll see about that ... I'm going to kill you ... Then I'll kill myself ..."

"But he's lying, Mother ... He said that because he doesn't like me ..."

"We'll see who doesn't like you ... The principal showed me the attendance book and you weren't in it ... I was ashamed like I've never been ashamed in my life ... I should have swallowed calomel instead of giving birth to you. You're exactly like your bastard of a father ... Oh, Lord above, to think that I sacrificed everything for you, Auguste ... Look at this black dress, I've been wearing the same one for ten years so I can pay for your schooling, and this is how you thank me ... Wait till we get to the house ..."

She burst into tears as she hammered away at Auguste's

head. Auguste stumbled as he went past our gallery.

"If that's the way it is ... If this is the path you've chosen, I might as well kill myself, and kill you first ... Oh, no, I won't leave you behind when I go ... I put you into this world ... I'll take you out of it ... Yes, I will ..."

She looked heavenward and beat her breast.

"Oh, Lord, I know it's my fault, my fault, all my fault ... *Mea culpa, mea culpa, mea maxima culpa* ... Oh, Da, I've been struck to my very soul ... You know, Da, how much I've sacrificed for this boy, and now I learn he hasn't been to school for a month ... Every day he gets up, gets washed, gets dressed, puts on the uniform I've spent all night washing and ironing because he only has one, then he has breakfast while I eat nothing, the slightest wisp of a wind would blow me away, Da, that's how weak I am, but he eats like a pig, then goes off to school ... Da, tell me what he's been doing every day for a month. Tell me, Da. My whole life, Da, has gone up in smoke ... And it hurts ... It hurts ... Right to my very soul ..."

"Sit down, Germaine, sit right here on the gallery ... That's right, my daughter ... I know how you feel ..."

Da looked at her for a time.

"Here, drink this ... It's Zoune's coffee."

28. SADNESS

THE WRONG WAY

Sylphise's mother arrived unexpectedly from Miragoâne and caught Rico on her gallery, talking with Sylphise. She hid her sweaty face under her big straw hat. No one saw her coming, not even Frantz, who was acting as lookout on his bicycle. She must have come along the seacoast, all the way from Petite Guinée. Frantz thought she would take the road behind the church.

THE HOODLUM

Sylphise's mother crossed the gallery without looking at anyone. As she went through the door, she turned around and discovered Sylphise.

"What are you doing here?"

"Nothing, Mother."

"Don't you have any lessons?"

"It's Friday, Mother."

"I know it's Friday, and don't talk back when I speak to you ..."

"I just got here, Mother."

"Oh, so you just got back ... I turn my back and you take advantage of it to come home any time you want to!"

"But, Mother, I was rehearsing with the choir ..."

"The choir, the choir, always the choir."

"I told you yesterday ..."

"What were you doing with that hoodlum?"

"I wasn't doing anything, Mother."

"You know I don't want to see you out on the streets with every hoodlum in this town."

"But, Mother ..."

"There are no 'buts' ... Go inside and wait for me."

Then she turned on Rico.

"As for you, you can just get off my gallery ... I don't want to see you here ever again ... You understand, don't you dare come back to my house, you little hoodlum."

Very slowly, Rico went down the little steps. With his head down. Sylphise's mother waited until he reached the middle of the street, then she went inside. No sooner had the door closed than we heard Sylphise's terrible screams.

"No, Mother ... No, Mother ... We weren't doing anything ..."

"Liar!"

BLACK SUN

Rico caught up with us. We walked down to the sea. Frantz rode into the water with his bicycle. If he doesn't clean it with Vaseline, the sea salt will eat up his spokes. We walked Rico to his house, staying along the shore. There was no breeze. The sea was motionless. Rico didn't say a word. Frantz tried to make him laugh by barking as if he were the dogfish. The sun had already set. We walked in darkness.

29. THE STRATEGY

THE CHAIN

Since it's Friday, Da let me go down to the main square.
Frantz was waiting for me.
"I need some money to get my chain fixed."
"What about your father?"
"Today, my father doesn't even know his own name."
That's how Frantz describes his father when he's drinking.
"I don't have any money, Frantz."
He smiled.
"I know where some is."
"But, Frantz ..."
"Don't worry, we won't rob anyone."
"How are we going to do it?"
"Follow me, you'll see."

THE SHOP

I understood as soon as I saw Zina in front of her mother's
shop. Zina will do anything Frantz desires. It's simple: she's
crazy about him.
"Now's the time," Frantz said to me, "go on ..."
"Me? Go where?"
"Don't you have ten centimes?"
"Sure."
"You don't have to do anything ... Just go into the shop
and buy something."

"Something?"

"A piece of candy, anything ..."

"Then what?"

"Shit, have you turned stupid on me? I told you: just do nothing."

"Just that?"

"Yes. Just that."

I played dumb to get on Frantz's nerves, but I understood as soon as I saw Zina in front of the shop.

MONEY

I was trembling a little as I went into the shop. I was afraid Zina's mother would show up and land on me, the way Sylphise's mother did with Rico. The difference is that Zina's mother wouldn't think twice about calling Sergeant Bazile. Zina was behind the counter. I bought a candy and paid for it.

"Did Frantz send you?"

"Yes. He's out there."

I nodded toward the street. She didn't speak. She opened the cash drawer and gave me a handful of coins. My two hands were full of money. I didn't know what to do. I was sweating bullets. My hands were shaking. What if Zina's mother showed up? I'd spend the rest of my days in prison.

"Tell him my mother has to go to Petite Guinée to run an errand ... I'll be waiting for him behind the church."

I was practically running when I left the shop. A few coins fell from my pocket onto the ground. I didn't stop to pick them up. I was sure everyone around me knew what I had done.

THE PRICE

We went to Wilson's immediately. Wilson is the only one

Frantz trusts for his bicycle. Wilson was eating. We waited for him in the hall. A little girl went past us, carrying a pitcher full of gasoline. Wilson came in, wiping his mouth with his shirt sleeve, then he squatted down to look at the bicycle.

"Your chain is finished."

"I know," said Frantz.

"What did you do to it?"

"I rode in the ocean ... How much will it cost?"

Wilson stood there and shook his head.

"You did that? You went into the ocean with a bike? What do you think it is? A boat? Are you crazy and just plain stupid?"

"Both. How much for the job, Wilson?"

Wilson kept his eyes down. He was still looking at the chain and shaking his head.

"The teeth are completely wrecked ... I'll have to cut them all over again ... When I think that you rode into the ocean with a bike! Do you know how many kids would like to have a bike like this one?"

"I don't know, Wilson ... I was sad ..."

Wilson got up heavily.

"You'll pay in advance, friend."

Wilson calls everyone "friend." Even his enemies. Once he said to Killick, "I'm going to have to tear your ears off your head, friend." He could have done it if Légype hadn't been there.

"Will you have it for this evening?" asked Frantz once he'd paid.

"You're nuts, friend. Fabrien's shop is closed already. I'll buy your chain tomorrow. You'll have your bicycle for tomorrow noon."

Wilson picked up the bicycle without a word and put it in the little dark storeroom behind the dining room. I was expecting some tough negotiations over the price.

"Why did you agree to his price without a fight, Frantz?"

"Wilson never bargains. If he doesn't want to fix a bicycle, he won't do it. Offer him all you want, it won't help."

THE MOTORBIKE

We still had a little money left. Légype took us down to the night market to see his mother who sells sugar cane there. The faces of the ladies behind their lamps. Légype tried to rob us. Frantz saw it coming and we left the market. On the way out, Wilson came speeding up on his old motorbike. He just missed us. Then he went on through the market. The cries of the frightened women. A litany of curses.

Sometimes, he takes his aged mother for a ride. She hangs onto his waist. One night, she fell off in the middle of the market. Wilson didn't notice she was gone until he stopped to greet Doctor Cayemitte, who asked after her.

BREASTS

Zina was waiting behind the church, sitting on the steps. It was dark, but you couldn't miss her white dress which was almost phosphorescent. Frantz went and sat next to her, and a few minutes later, I saw them go behind Professor Casamé's little clump of trees. I can't say that Frantz kissed her, but I do know he's done worse to Sylphise. He even felt her breasts. Sylphise has big breasts. Zina scarcely has any at all. It's not her fault, but that's the way it is. They stayed in there a pretty long time. I would have given anything to know what they were doing, in the stillness, in the dark. Finally, when Zina came past me, she was almost running. She had the face of someone who had been crying. Frantz walked me back home and I went in to bed. Da stayed up on the gallery, talking with Zette.

PART VI

30. THAT FATEFUL MORNING

BREAKFAST

Zina went to Sylphise's house early. She sat down at the table to watch her eat breakfast. Bread and coffee. Zina loves the aroma of coffee. Even when you don't drink it, its aroma finds its way into your bones. The coffee that Sylphise drinks is not very good. Her mother mixes water with her coffee. A girl shouldn't drink strong coffee, her mother says. Sylphise casually dunked her bread in her coffee. A piece of soggy bread stayed behind in the cup. Zina never mixes that way. She eats her bread dry and drinks her coffee afterward. What she loves most of all is very strong, very sweet coffee, followed by a cup of ice-cold water, drunk slowly. She thought of all these things as she watched Sylphise dawdle over her breakfast. Sylphise didn't seem to have a care in the world. She hadn't even done her homework, even though she'd had all weekend to do it. Zina took out her notebooks and put them on the table, next to Sylphise.

THE LITTLE BENCH

Zina and Sylphise met up with Didi near the Rigauds' big wooden house, where the tragic fire took place, last year. Didi came up the rue La-Paix, from the opposite direction. Didi lives near the sisters' school, but every morning she meets them at the same place, halfway to Zina's and Sylphise's house. The Rigaud house is at the middle of the triangle whose three angles are formed by Zina's, Didi's and Sylphise's houses. Usually they sit a moment on the little bench on the Rigaud gallery to catch their breath.

THE PAPER

"Did you have time to finish the paper?"

"Yes," said Zina.

"What paper?" asked Sylphise.

"Sylphise, didn't you know we had a paper to write on Galbaud's accident?"

"What accident?"

Didi and Zina raised their arms heavenward.

"What accident?" Sylphise asked again.

"The accident," Didi and Zina answered in unison.

Sylphise opened her eyes wide.

"Galbaud's accident. He fell into the ocean with his car."

"Nobody told me anything about it ... Zina, why didn't you tell me this morning?"

"No way. I already got a zero once because you wrote the same thing I did."

"That's normal, Zina. We see things the same way."

Everyone laughed. Even Sylphise.

"Zina," said Sylphise, "I don't have time for jokes. I have to have that paper."

The stream of students started to swell. Didi waved to her friends who passed by in the street.

"No, Sylphise, I told you, it's personal. Anyway, Sister Noel said that since we're not twins ..."

"I don't give a damn about Sister Noel. The paper's for Miss Lezeska."

"So, say you weren't here this weekend ... Tell her your mother took you to Miragoâne ..."

"No, tell her you don't know anything about the harbor instead," Didi interrupted.

"Don't be stupid, Didi, Sister Noel will never swallow that."

"Oh, God, my head hurts."

"Don't start in with that, Sylphise, it'll never work with me, I know you too well ... You'll never get my paper that way."

"If you start whimpering now," said Didi, "you'll never think of an excuse for Sister Noel ... And God only knows you need one this morning."

"I'm not kidding ... It's true, I don't feel well ... Didi, it's so nasty of you to say that ... Just leave me alone, both of you ... I feel terrible and that's all you can say ... Go away, I don't want to see either of you."

"Here, you can have my paper, but try not to write the exact same thing ... I don't want to end up at the principal's office again."

THE ANTHEM

They set out again, making sure they would arrive just as Sister Noel went onto the balcony to ring the bell. The girls poured into the schoolyard. Sister Noel made her presence felt immediately. First came silence, then the national anthem.

> *Pour le pays*
> *pour les ancêtres*
> *marchons unis ...*

A fat girl used the occasion to box Sylphise's ears. Vava turned around just in time to see Philomena withdraw her hand. Zina gave Philomena a swift kick. The girl next to her slapped Zina in the head.

Marchons unis
Dans nos rangs, point de traîtres.
Du sol, soyons seuls maîtres.

Sister Noel saw everything. She pinched her lips that were as thin as razor blades. Her eyes threw daggers. She went on beating time with her big ruler, keeping her eyes on the group. Then it was over. Everyone went into the classroom.

"The five of you, over there, go to the principal's office and wait for me there."

"I didn't do anything," Didi protested.

"I know. But as far as I can tell, your friends did," the sister answered with a mixture of irony and cruelty.

THE GROUP

Didi, Vava, Zina and Sylphise, for better or for worse. In the middle of them all: handsome Frantz.

Didi looked out the classroom window at a cow going by. It gave her a sad smile.

3 1. G O D

Brother Simon came into the classroom with his greasy cassock and his dirty nails. He smells like a goat that's been smoking tobacco. Brother Simon comes from Brittany. He teaches French. Brother Simon has the unpleasant habit of making us pray in silence as soon as he comes into the classroom. We kneel down on our seats. Heads bowed. In silence. Suddenly there's the cry of a bird. Everyone turns toward the window. Another cry. Brother Simon listens hard. The cry comes from among us. The Brother walks down the rows, looking each one of us straight in the eye. The cry is more piercing now. The Brother pivots and grabs Rico by the scruff of the neck. He opens his desk. A poor, stunned-looking little bird looks up at the Brother, then releases another dreadful cry. We can see the back of its throat and its tiny tongue all but stuck to its palate.

SMELLS

"What's this bird doing here?"

"I don't know, Brother," Rico tells him.

"Are you absolutely sure?"

"I don't know, Brother."

"Well, if you don't, can you name me someone who does?"

"I don't know, Brother."

I look at Brother Simon's square jaw from close up. He brushes me with his cassock, that smells of piss and tobacco. I'm very sensitive to smells. I have to stop breathing, otherwise I'll faint dead away.

"I don't know, Brother."

"Well, I know what it's doing there, and I'm going to tell you ..."

"It's singing, Brother."

"No, it's dying because you hid it in your desk. But you're going to take it with you to the principal's office."

Poor Rico.

WHAT IS GOD?

Brother Hervé always tells us we must understand what we recite. Man is a reasoning animal. We must not repeat everything like parrots. Brother Hervé teaches religion.

"I'm going to ask you the simplest and most important question in all of religion ... First, what is that question?"

No one answers. Brother Hervé always does that. He wants us to tell him the question he's going to ask us. That's how he teaches. We wait for a couple of minutes. He watches us with a little smile on his lips. I've always thought that Brother Hervé was a perfect idiot.

"What is God?—that's the question. What is God, Bernadotte?"

Bernadotte is a poor idiot who's always number one in class. One day, Frantz punched him out, just because of that. "Aren't you sick and tired of being number one?" Bernadotte hid in the toilet to cry. Next month, he was number two. It was the first time he wasn't at the top of the class.

"God is pure spirit ..." Bernadotte began.

"Stop right there. God is pure spirit," he said dreamily.

"That's more than enough for one day."

We started to pick up our things.

"What's that noise?" Brother Hervé thundered. "I didn't dismiss the class ... God is pure spirit—that's enough to occupy our mediocre minds ... Thank you, Bernadotte ... Now, Lochard, tell us what a pure spirit is?"

Lochard stood up. He was number one the time that Bernadotte wasn't. Bernadotte and he study together. They live at the top of the street, near the Devieux house, just before you cross the river.

"A pure spirit is a spirit without stain."

"Not bad ... It's true that a pure spirit is without stain, but that's not quite it, Lochard. Let's just say that that's not quite enough ..."

It's my turn. I'm sitting next to Lochard. He's going to point at me. What is a pure spirit? *A bird on the wing,* I feel like telling him.

"Coutard, what do you think of all this?"

He skipped over me. Frantz wasn't expecting it.

"A pure spirit is a pure spirit."

Laughter in the classroom.

"You simple-minded ..."

Then he pointed at me.

"You tell us what a pure spirit is."

I stand up slowly, with a smile. I open my mouth in slow motion. The bell rings.

32. THE MAD CYCLIST

Frantz went to pick up his bicycle in the clump of bushes by the fountain. He saw Bernadotte's bicycle, and Philibert's, and Lochard's, but not his. Strange, because he leaves his there every day, leaning against the low wall that separates the schoolyard from the Laviolettes' garden. There is a big dog behind the wall whose job is to start barking when anyone tries to get in. The mangos in that garden are excellent. Once, Frantz jumped over the wall. The dog came rushing at him, yapping like crazy. Frantz gave it such a kick in the chops that we had a week's worth of peace afterward. Who took Frantz's bicycle? Certainly not the dog; it starts whimpering every time it sees him.

THE MADMAN

Who would have stolen such a junk heap? No one, except for Aurélien. Frantz saw him riding by, his hands on his head, pedaling along with a smile. Aurélien wasn't always crazy. He used to be an honest mason who worked for Desroches. One day, he started telling people how he had punched a donkey and killed it. They began to tease him about it. He didn't like that at all. Instead of laughing, he got angry. And that's when everything started going wrong. He began throwing rocks at people. Kids started shouting, "Hee-haw! Hee-haw!" whenever they saw him, and that's why, one day, he left everything—his trade, his wife, his children—to take to the streets, day and night, pursuing those who had mocked him with donkey noises.

THE RACE

Frantz ran after Aurélien, who turned right onto the rue Dessalines. The bicycle rode past Maurice Bonhomme's private school and went right into the market. It was the middle of the day. The vendors leaped this way and that, opening a clear path for him. Frantz stayed right behind him. Aurélien turned left and set off toward the barracks. He was moving at such speed that the soldier on duty in his guardhouse, under the coconut palm, didn't have time to stop him. A sergeant ran up, and with no questions asked, took the bicycle from Aurélien's grasp and gave it back to Frantz.

"You promised me you wouldn't do that again," Sergeant Bazile said.

Aurélien bowed his head.

"Didn't you promise me?"

Aurélien made a move to leave.

"Where do you think you're going?"

He pointed toward the market.

"Stay. You can eat with us."

"All right, as long as I can leave afterward."

"Has anyone ever kept you here against your will?"

Sergeant Bazile motioned to Aurélien to follow him. A group of soldiers came marching into the barracks yard. A prisoner walked along behind with a large platter of bananas and fried fish on his head.

33. DEATH

Sylphise was sitting on the little bench at the Rigaud house.
Her head on Zina's shoulder. Her eyes were closed.

Frantz arrived two minutes after I did.

"I can drop her off, Zina."

Sylphise lifted her head ever so slightly and gave a weak
smile.

"No, Frantz," said Zina. "Her headache's too bad. She
can't go on a bike."

"What are you going to do then?"

"We'll wait till Devieux's chauffeur comes by and I'll
ask him to drop us off at Sylphise's house … He's her
mother's cousin."

"What if he doesn't come by?"

"He always does."

THE MADWOMAN

Da made ground corn. It gives me a stomach-ache. Every
time I eat ground corn I get terrible cramps. Still, I love
the stuff. With a good hot sauce and two slices of avocado.
A purple avocado that Da bought from a woman in Petite
Guinée. I never tell Da that corn gives me a stomache-ache;
otherwise, she won't make it any more. I try to eat slowly,
because I've noticed that it's worse when I eat too fast. I look
out the window as I eat. The dining-room window looks

onto the park. I see Miracine the madwoman go by. She's dressed all in black. A chamber-pot on her head for a hat. Her long, tangled braids, full of mud, reach down to her waist. Miracine screams her death cry.

"Ah! Ah! Ah! Curses rain upon our heads. Curses upon the children of Israel! Babylon, Babylon, Babylon, three times Babylon, Babylon the Great, you shall devour your own entrails, Babylon, you shall weep tears of blood ... Ah! Ah!"

THE NEWS

Zette opened her window.

"What's wrong, Miracine?"

"Big Simon just won the grand prize."

"Glory to God!"

"And his daughter died at the same time."

"Satan himself!"

The window slammed shut.

DEATH

I left my plate on the table. I don't know how long I sat there, motionless. Oginé came into the park with Naréus' horse which started whinnying, and almost kicked Miracine. Miracine ran off, cursing, frothing at the mouth. Frantz came by a little later. We walked to the soccer field. No one was there. No players. Frantz picked up a rock and threw it very high into the sky. It landed in the yard of the sisters' school. The guard came out. We played dumb. A bird flew past us, calling at the top of its lungs. We walked straight to the sea.

PART VII

3 4. WHAT LIFE IS
MADE OF

A CLOUD

Doctor Cayemitte climbed down from Big Simon's truck, in front of our gallery. Big Simon stopped by to congratulate Da for finally having the roof painted.

"Da, you can't imagine the good you've done. I was about to scratch the rue Lamarre off my route. And that's impossible, seeing as I always have merchandise to drop off for the Syrian or Abraham."

Da shrugged her shoulders.

"Da, I have a letter for you."

Big Simon handed the letter to Doctor Cayemitte, who passed it on to Da. Big Simon climbed back into his truck, which creaked off slowly. The new truck. Marquis rushed after the truck's big tires, with his claws out. A little cloud of dust swallowed up Marquis.

THE SMELL OF IODINE

I've always loved Doctor Cayemitte's smell. He smells of the tincture of iodine he spends all day preparing in the back of his pharmacy on the rue Pétion. His fingertips are always red. I opened my mouth. He put his big finger on my tongue and inspected the inside of my throat. Then he examined my eyes, asking me to look right, then left.

Doctor Cayemitte turned to Da with a smile.

"What this boy needs, Da, is some exercise."

Da stared at him, unbelieving.

"And you waited till the end of vacation to tell me that, Doctor?"

"What vacation?"

"Summer vacation," Da said with a worried voice.

Doctor Cayemitte slapped himself on the forehead.

"That's why they're always underfoot all day long!"

A moment went by.

"In that case, have him take his vacation during the school year."

"Are you feeling quite well, Doctor?"

"Let this boy run free, Da, that's the only medicine he needs. Well, I have to be going now ... I have a chess game with Loné and the clever devil never gives me a break."

Doctor Cayemitte stepped down from our gallery, then walked back and handed Da the little bottle of yellow piss.

"Everything is fine, Da. This boy is ready to learn all the stupidities that will be crammed into his head, whether he likes it or not."

"Which is how a man becomes a doctor later in life."

Doctor Cayemitte was still laughing when he turned the corner toward Loné the notary's house, on the rue Desvignes.

THE LETTER

The letter came from my mother. She sent a little money for my school expenses. I need a new bag. Da will buy one from Fabrien, along with the red bicycle she promises me every year. My mother wrote her letter in pencil. It's hard to read. Da can't see well enough to read it. I have to do it for her. Aunt Ninine found a job at the post office. She sells stamps to collectors. Aunt Gilberte is teaching at a small school at Source Matelas, not too far from Port-au-Prince.

She spends the weekdays there. Aunt Raymonde isn't working yet. Neither is Aunt Renée. My mother says she's sending the money for pencils, a ruler, notebooks and penholders. She'll buy the books herself at Deschamps and Madame Midi will make me the weekday uniform and the little Sunday suit for Mass. The rest of the money will go for sundry expenses. She sends her love and kisses to Da and me.

THE MARE

Oginé went by with Chaël Charles' mare, which was ready to drop her colt. Naréus flew into a rage when he heard the news. The mare walked with her back legs slightly spread. With her tail, she shooed the flies that stung at her eyes. The sky began to grow darker. Naréus' ducks crossed the street and waddled slowly into Cornélia's yard. The mare's shoe almost crushed a duckling. The mother duck turned around to scold the mare.

ANTS

Every time it's about to rain, I notice that the ants are busier. They have to bring in the merchandise quickly, otherwise, they'll be ruined. Even the flying ants help out, though normally, they do nothing all day. Zette gathers her washing. The ants rub noses when they meet. Whenever there is a death among them, they take up position around the cadaver until the stretcher-bearers arrive to carry it down into the hole.

SUNSHINE AFTER A RAIN

Da didn't even have time to bring in her chair, and already the sun is out again. The ants pour happily from their hole.

With their customary febrility, they take up the work interrupted by the rain. The damage was serious. A piece of brick that supported the anthill was washed away. People pass by, telling the story of Big Simon and his daughter.

"Some people will do anything for money," said Thérèse.

"Yes, daughter."

THE GAME

Auguste comes up the street with a new ball, followed by a dozen players, most of whom come from Petite Guinée. Camelo is going to coach them. They go straight to the big field, around behind Batichon's house. I watch them walk, their legs well spread because of their spiked shoes.

LIZARD

A green lizard lying by Da's chair. It feigns sleep, better to catch a fly. Da serves herself a cup of coffee. A drop of hot coffee falls on the lizard's head. It skitters off toward the park.

THE AFTERNOON ENDS

No one in the street. Except Marquis coming up the slope, practically dancing.

35. THE WINDOW

The first time Loné the notary stepped through his window, it was simply because he had forgotten his key. He was astonished at the intense pleasure he experienced. Yet, despite it, he did not repeat the action that day.

Two days later, Loné the notary, returning from his daily stroll, attempted entry through his window again. Unfortunately, it was a Saturday, and the street was crowded with people.

By the following week, Loné the notary had completely lost the habit of going through the door to get into his house.

After a month of this regimen, someone finally reported his strange behavior to Zette, who mentioned it to Da. The next day, the entire town was aware of it.

On a Thursday afternoon in the middle of the month of September, the people gathered near Loné the notary's house to await him. He was returning from a chess game with Passilus. The notary walked calmly toward his house. He climbed the steps onto his gallery and, spontaneously, moved toward the window. Then he stopped himself. For the first time, he thought of resuming his old method of simply walking through the door. The notary hesitated at length, then made the fatal decision to step up to the window. As he was about to go through it, he turned around. There was no one in the street. The people had all found hiding places: behind the trees, in the houses, on the roofs, in the tall grass.

Not a sound could be heard.

Then, light of foot, Loné the notary of the rue Desvignes stepped through his window. One too many times.

3 6. TIME

Augereau didn't even have time to say hello to Da, and already she was offering him a cup of coffee. Augereau refused, saying that Da would have no desire to offer him anything once he'd spoken.

"Something's happened in Port-au-Prince?"

"No, Da."

"Tell me if one of my daughters ..."

"No, Da."

"Augereau, I'll never forgive you if you don't tell me the truth ... Gilberte or Raymonde had an accident. It can't be Renée because yesterday I saw her friend Antoine, and he ..."

"No, Da. I said no. Nothing happened to any of your daughters ... At least as far as I know."

"Ah! Now, you're starting to talk."

"That's what I've been trying to tell you Da, ever since I got here."

"So then, Augereau, what's the catastrophe?"

"The house, Da."

"What's the matter with it? Oh, I know, it leaks, last week I asked Absence to come and look after it ... The next time he comes to buy cane liquor at Mozart's, I'll ask him again ..."

"No, Da. Bombace sent me."

"Ah! That vulture ... I knew it ... He's been circling

around me for a while now … What does he want, Augereau? He wants to buy the house."

"No, Da."

"What? Augereau, you're keeping something from me."

"He already bought it, Da."

Da said nothing.

"The father sold it. He needed money to build his still."

There was a long silence.

"So that was it! I suspected it. I always wondered where he got that money. He told me he'd sold his land on The Plains. At least we'll have the still."

Augereau shook his head.

"No, Da. He had to borrow more money from Bombace, which means the still belongs to Bombace too."

"And now you, my son, have come here to tell me this. I saw you go past my gallery when you weren't even five years old. You would run past, naked as Adam. And now, today, you stab me in the back."

Augereau looked at the ground.

"No, Da, I'm not stabbing you in the back. I'd give ten years of my life not to have to do what I'm doing now. Da, you're part of my life. You watched me grow up. My mother used to say, 'Da is on her gallery as sure as the sun rises in the morning.' And my father would answer with a laugh, 'Surer still, because we don't see the sun every day.' All my life, Da, you've been at this same spot … That's important for me … More important than my job at the Maison Bombace …"

"Thank you, Augereau … That's all well and good, but here I am without a roof over my head, and my grandson who's sick. What should I do now, Augereau?"

An ant had time to go from Da's chair to the old scale.

"Just sit here, Da. As long as you're sitting, no one can make you move. The mountain doesn't move. Act like you don't know anything."

"And you, my son?"

"I'll make my report. I'll say I warned you. That's my job: to warn you. Nothing else."

Another silence. Da breathed in a good lungful of air, sat back deeper in her chair and, for the briefest second, closed her eyes.

"Care for a cup of coffee, Augereau?"

"Gladly, Da."

Augereau breathed in the aroma of the coffee before he took his first sip. Everything else is just a matter of time.

37. THE WORLD

Every day, the black car comes past, the opposite way, around six in the evening. The passenger sitting in the back seat is my age. Old Devieux had a son, and his son had a son too. The youngest is returning from the store. I always see him in profile. He sits very straight. Staring ahead. He's ten years old, as I am. Da says that makes four generations of Devieuxs she's watched going past her gallery.

The world has changed, says Da, but the Devieuxs remain the same.

38. THE BOOK

(THIRTY YEARS LATER)

I wrote this book for all sorts of reasons.

To praise the coffee (the coffee of Les Palmes) that Da loved so well, and to speak of Da, whom I loved too.

So I would never forget that dragonfly covered with ants.

Nor the smell of the earth.

Nor the rains of Jacmel.

Nor the sea beyond the coconut palms.

Nor the evening breeze.

Nor Vava, and the fire of first love.

Nor the merciless noontime sun.

Nor Auguste, Frantz, Rico, my childhood friends.

Nor Didi, my cousin, nor Zina, nor Sylphise, the dead child, nor even my faithful Marquis.

I wrote this book especially for that one scene that haunted me for so long: a young boy sitting at his grandmother's feet on a sunlit gallery in a small provincial town.

Goodnight, Da!